I0772909

ALAN VAN ORMER

Hidden in the Book

Book 3: Mystery of the Hunt

Alan Van Ormer

ISBN-13: 978-1-965352-20-5

Contents

THE MYSTERY OF THE HUNT

The young woman stopped to catch her breath. A twenty-two-year-old should be able to scramble up the side of Mount Stimson without a problem. That's what she deserved for agreeing to join her boyfriend for the annual Mystery Hunt in the Rocky Mountains of Montana.

They were transported up to a 9,000-foot site that included several cabins, a beautiful lake, and an enormous amount of trees and trails. The first night had been a lot of fun with dancing, singing, and drinking, but early in the morning, everything changed. She and her boyfriend were the only ones left.

Now, seven hours later, she was the only survivor after her boyfriend had fallen into a deep hole. From her vantage point, the unnatural angle of his head and eyes that stared at nothing let her know it was useless to go get help. Was this hole part of the mystery hunt?

Her head snapped to the left at the taunting noises once more. She took off running as fast as she could, but the edge of a cliff came too fast. The last thing she heard was her own screams as she tumbled down from the edge.

Chapter 1

Allison Winters giggled at her boyfriend, Chase Connor. "I thought you knew everything there was to know about boats."

He lifted his head toward her and scowled. "I never said anything about knowing everything about boats."

She laughed once more at the black ooze that spit at his face. "I'm sorry. You just look so cute trying to start the engine. Do you need my help?"

"If you would be so kind."

She snickered and joined him. "What do you want me to do?"

"Can you hold this thingy-gadget so I can tighten it?"

"Thingy-gadget? You mean the gear?"

Chase simpered. "I just wanted to see if you knew what it was."

"Right." Allison bent down to hold the gear while he tightened it. Once completed, he stepped back. "Ta da. We fixed it."

She kissed him on the forehead. "I knew you could do it."

"Now let's hope it starts." He pulled the cord, and

the motor kicked right in.

"I love it," Allison said. "It's official. You do know a little about boats."

"Thanks. Do you want to navigate while I clean up?"

"I can do that. We're not too far from the cabin my dad purchased with your help."

While Chase cleaned off the grease from his hands and face, she headed toward the cabin which was on the northside of Smith Lake. Her blonde hair whipped across her face as the boat made its way toward her father's cabin. The wind rippled her shorts and oversized button-down shirt.

Allison glanced back at Chase who was still cleaning off the grease. "Why would your brother Micah tell Sheriff Portal that my father helped solve the mystery of Bigfoot, when Micah knew that my dad was criminally involved all along?"

He threw the greasy rag on the boat's floor and joined her. "Micah knew how important you were to me."

"I appreciate what he did, but if my father was involved, he should pay the price."

Chase scrubbed a spot on his forehead. "Remember, your father really had no choice because he was protecting his family."

She steered the boat toward the dock, which was on the horizon. "Do you believe there are other seven-foot freaks out there in the Rocky Mountains?"

"Possibly, but Jonathan Gartner won't be using them for his elaborate drug-operating scheme because he'll be spending a long time in jail. I can't believe it took so long for law enforcement to figure out that he was using human mules to transport drugs. What are your feelings about your former boyfriend, Willis, and his father being indicted in the scheme?"

"When I hooked up with you several months ago, I put Willis and his family out of my mind. After you hired me as the bookstore manager and allowed me to live in the upstairs apartment, what else could a woman want?"

Chase wrapped his arms around her, then turned her around, and lifted her head up to kiss him. She gazed at his light brown hair blowing in the wind and his striking blue eyes, then pulled his shades down. "No grease on your face."

"I'm just glad to get the boat running. I would hate to row to the cabin or call someone to come bail us out."

Once they were near the dock, Allison jumped off the boat onto the landing to hook up the rope. As she was winding it around the cleat in a figure-eight pattern, Allison glanced up to see two young girls running toward the dock. Melanie and Melody scampered toward them.

A voice hollered from behind. "Slow down, you two."

Allison grabbed her two nieces. "Okay you two, be careful. I'd hate for you to fall into the water because your Uncle Chase would have to dive in to save you. I'm not sure he knows how to swim, so you might have to save him."

The two girls giggled. "Come on, Aunt Allison, if he owns a boat he knows how to swim."

Allison's sister, Haley, joined them. Her blonde hair puffed in the wind. "The twins are excited about seeing you, Allison."

"When did you get in?"

"We arrived last night to spend a few days with Dad. I can't believe how much he's changed. I hope that means he's in a much better place in his life."

Allison set the twins down. "He is, and I'm happy for him. How's Garrett?"

"He's sitting in the cabin with Dad talking about fishing and hunting. I learned something new about my husband after five years."

Haley switched her attention to Chase who had climbed onto the dock. "So, this is your boyfriend?"

Allison linked her arm with Chase's. "Yes, this is Chase."

"Nice to meet you," Chase said. "And these must be your two children?"

Haley nodded. "Melody and Melanie are twins."

Chase winked. "Two beauties like their mom."

They both giggled. "We're only five, but we know we're cute," Melody, the taller of the two, said. "Dad tells us that all the time."

"Got ya."

Haley interrupted. "Dad and Garrett are in the cabin. Chase, our father is a stickler for being on time, and it's time for lunch." As they followed her up the trail, Haley glanced back over her shoulder. "Dad made up some kind of salad for lunch. He's big into salads."

They arrived at the cabin. Chase opened the door for the gals. "Quite the gentleman," Haley grinned.

Allison smiled. "That and more."

"I can tell," her sister said.

Her father, whose hair had whitened in the last few months took off his readers, stood and hugged Allison, then shifted his glance toward Chase. "Welcome. I'm Ethan Winters. You're just in time for lunch. I've made my famous big mac pasta salad. Have a seat."

They all sat down around a wooden table with a bench on each side. The two young girls slipped in between their mom and dad. Allison's brother-in-law stuck out his hand. "I'm Garrett. You must be Chase?"

"I am. Nice to meet you, Garrett."

Chase and Allison sat down next to each other as her dad dished out the salad.

"Any small pasta works like small shells, rotini or penne. I chose boiled diced potatoes, which is different from the way most cooks make the salad. Dig in."

Chase took his first bite. "This is very good, Mr. Winters."

"I'm glad you enjoy it."

They spent the next hour eating and chatting. "Any word on the resort?" Chase asked.

Ethan put down his fork. "Haven't heard any more on it. I'll be driving south to Wyoming for another possible site. In a way I hope it doesn't happen in Montana because this land is beautiful and I'd hate to see it ruined with construction."

Garrett jumped in. "Aren't there enough resorts in Montana?"

Chase shook his head. "Resorts are moneymakers and provide jobs for county residents, so it's probably safe to say there is no limit to projects."

Ethan grabbed another bite of his pasta and turned to Chase. "Any new mysteries you're searching for from the books?"

"I'm always reading, so something will come up. I did have a gal in Whitefish tell me about a mystery hunt somewhere in the mountains above Smith Lake, but I've never heard about it, at least not yet."

Haley peered at Allison. "What part do you play in all of this, Allison?"

She sampled her lemonade then put her glass down. "Chase usually works with the sheriff, but if he needs my help, I'm always willing to jump in."

Everyone helped with the cleanup. The twins stayed with their grandfather while the others went for a hike along a trail.

"I'm thankful I'm walking on one of these mountain trails in the summer," Chase said.

Garrett looked at Allison. "What is he talking about?"

"He's not a big fan of snow."

They walked for another hour before they stopped at a higher elevation where they could see for a long distance.

Allison linked her arm in Chase's. "This is beautiful," she said. "I've lived in Montana all my life, and I've never taken the time to see such things. Thank you." She reached up and kissed him.

Haley agreed. "It is gorgeous. Look at the eagle flying through the sky."

They all gazed at where Haley was pointing. Chase pulled out his phone to take a photo of the majestic bird. Once he took a few shots he looked at them. "I got one in focus."

The others looked at the photo.

Garrett scoffed. "I saw a photo of an eagle lifting a full-grown deer on my cell phone the other day. Now that's amazing!"

They stood there staring at the scenery for another

thirty minutes until Allison broke the silence. She leaned forward and pointed. "Is that a body?"

Chase pulled out binoculars out of his backpack searching where Allison's finger was pointed. "It sure looks like it. Let's check it out."

They made the slow trek down the trail taking twenty minutes to get to the body. Chase bent down. "She has a faint pulse."

Haley whipped around, her eyes scanning the trees. "What is it?" her husband asked.

"I feel eyes gawking at us."

Garrett searched the area. "I don't see anything."

Chase interrupted. "We have to get her help now. There's no service this high."

Garrett jumped in. "I'll hightail it to where I can get service and call for help. Can you carry her?"

Chase lifted her. "I think so. She's pretty light."

Allison added. "She doesn't look like she's eaten for a while. Maybe it would be better if Haley and I head down the mountain to call for help."

"Go," Chase said.

She reached up to kiss him. "Please be safe."

"I'll meet you at the cabin."

The two women walked quickly, keeping their eyes alert.

"You think a lot of Chase," her sister said.

Allison brushed hair out of her eyes. "I do."

"Are you two getting married?"

"We haven't talked about it, but someday I'll marry him."

"You two go well together."

They slowed their pace to catch their breath. Allison peered at her sister. "You don't seem happy with Garrett."

Haley blew out a breath. "Things have changed over the last year. He's not happy with his job, wants to get out, but he's not sure what he wants to do. Now he's talking about moving here to work as a fishing and hunting guide."

"You don't like the idea?"

Haley stepped around a log. "He knows nothing about either, and that's just it—he changes his mind like the weather."

They quickened up the pace once more. Allison broke the silence. "Chase is an attorney by trade, a very good one, but he wasn't happy with who he had become, so he took a shot and bought a bookstore, then an antique store. The guy has been happy and successful so far. I wouldn't want it any other way."

"That isn't me."

Allison stopped to see if they had service. She did. She dialed 9-1-1.

A woman's voice on the other end answered. "What's your emergency?"

"A young lady barely breathing with a badly broken leg." Allison gave her the location as best she could.

The last thing the emergency operator said was, "We'll be there as soon as possible."

Allison pivoted to head back.

"Where are you going?" Haley asked.

"I'm going to help Chase. You can go back to the cabin."

"That's where I'm headed."

Allison watched as Haley hurried toward the trail. Once her sister was around the bend, she hastened her step back up the mountain. Throughout the trip back to Chase, Allison felt eyes staring at her. Occasionally she stopped to survey the area but didn't see anything. She finally saw Chase and Garrett and hurried toward them. "Can I do anything to help?"

"Did you contact the emergency responders?"

"They're on their way."

She touched his face. "Are you okay?"

He moaned. "It's hard to imagine someone this small being this heavy."

Garrett jumped in "I'll take her for a bit."

After Garrett lifted her up, they continued on. Chase slipped his arm around Allison's shoulders.

She squeezed his hand. "What do you think of this?"

"We won't know until she wakes up, if she does. She's struggling to breathe. It appears she fell from above or was pushed." He pivoted and told Garrett to be on the lookout for the EMS workers.

"Wow." She stopped.

"What?"

She took a deep breath. "You're going back up there?"

Chase nodded. They started walking again.

"I'm going with you."

"I don't think so."

She stopped once more, placing her hands on his face. "Don't tell me I'm not. I'd rather be *with* you than worrying about you."

Chapter 2

"How come whenever there's something happening in Flathead County, you're right in the middle of it?"

Sheriff Lancaster Portal was a bit shorter than Chase's six-one frame, but today he appeared taller to Chase because of the angry look on his face.

"We were just hiking."

The sheriff snarled. "Why couldn't you be hiking elsewhere?"

Chase couldn't help but laugh. "I'm sorry, but do you hear yourself? Something else on your mind?"

The sheriff surveyed the area. "Yeah, Gartner and the Shepherds are claiming they were illegally arrested."

"How can that be? They threatened to kill me and told me about what they were doing."

The sheriff pulled off his hat to wipe his brow. "I don't know what's going to happen. They've brought in some big shot attorneys from around the state. Right now, they're arguing about having to post a bond. They're blaming my department saying we're incompetent and corrupt. Enough about them. Let's take a walk to see what we can find."

"One moment." Chase hurried over to Allison, who was with her family. Her eyes were wide as she reached for his hands. "Is everything okay?"

"The sheriff wants me to take him back to where we found the body. I know you wanted to join me."

She reached up, wrapped her arms around his neck, and gave him a sweet kiss. "Go. I'll wait for you. I love you."

"Ditto."

~

Once he left, Allison's father put his arms around her shoulders. "Do you worry about him?"

She glanced at his profile. "Every moment, but I wouldn't have it any other way because he's doing what he loves. Still it's hard when he goes off like this. I never know if he's going to come back."

Ethan sipped on his beer. "I can tell you care a lot about him."

"No question. He's everything I hoped for in a guy. The one big problem is he believes he's not good enough for me because he's a Connor. I keep telling him he's nothing like his family."

Her father drank his beer. "Peter Drake told me some things about what happened to him. It wasn't pleasant."

Allison glowered. "What did he tell you?"

"That Chase has loved several girls, his family is tough to deal with, and he's interested in this resort."

"Dad, I've loved other guys, or at least thought I did, but Chase is the first man I've been in love with. He feels the same way about me." The water tasted cool going down her throat. "He told me about his family before I met them, but they were kind to me. Can they be nasty? Yes, I've seen that in my parents. No matter what Peter Drake says, Chase wants nothing to do with the resort. I guarantee that."

"I hope you know what you're doing."

"I do because he makes me feel loved, special; no other guy has ever done that."

Her cell phone vibrated. It was Sophia Shepherd.

"Excuse me, Dad." Allison stepped away from her father. She hadn't heard from Sophia in several months. The two had been best friends, and then Sophia had moved to Boston with her fiancé, Kirby Hall, a former detective for Flathead County.

"Sophia, how have you been?"

"Doing well. I had heard about the situation with Willis, and I wanted to make sure you were okay."

"I'm better, thanks to Chase."

Silence on the other end. "How is he doing?"

Allison laughed. "Up to his neck in helping the sheriff solve some cases."

Sophia laughed also. "For a man who wants to run a bookstore, he sure gets mixed up in the wildest things."

"That's true. How's Kirby?"

Again, silence before Sophia answered. "I'll tell you when I get to Montana. I'll fly to Kalispell in a couple of days. Mom is cracking under all this stuff with my dad and brother, so I'm going to help her out."

"Do you have a place to stay? If not, you can stay here in the extra bedroom at the bookstore. Chase wouldn't mind."

"Thanks. I'll probably just stay with my mom."

"It'll be great to see you. I have a lot of things to

tell you also."

"Tell Chase hi for me."

"I'll do that."

After Allison hung up the phone, she took a deep breath. What was she worried about? If Chase asked her to marry him, she would say yes. Still, there was something gnawing at her. Her woman's intuition was telling her not to trust her friend.

~

It was twenty minutes before the sheriff took a breather. "I'm really getting tired of climbing these mountains."

"Why don't you get the rescue crews to do it?"

He smirked. "And miss all the fun? Let's move."

They climbed for ten more minutes when Chase stopped. "It was right around here."

The two searched for any type of sign but found nothing. "There's not even any signs of blood," the sheriff said.

Chase didn't say anything but kept searching. He started walking to the north when he saw another body at the bottom of the ravine. "Sheriff, another body. This one's dead."

They headed down toward the body, his head twisted at an unnatural angle. The sheriff knelt down. "It looks like his neck was broken and he died immediately. If I had to guess, he was with the young lady we found earlier."

"That would make sense. They must have been traveling in the darkness. Something must have scared them. But what?"

The sheriff surveyed the area. "It could have been a grizzly or another wild animal. But my guess is humans."

"Why would you say that?"

"Just a feeling."

Chase snapped his fingers. "The mystery hunt."

Sheriff Portal looked confused. "What are you talking about?"

"Each year a group of people go high into the mountains to participate in some kind of hunt. The only reason I know about it is because a bartender in Whitefish told me about it. She even wrote down the name of someone who had been contacted but chose not to participate."

Sheriff Portal winced. "Leah Furness, the bartender in Whitefish?"

"I didn't catch her name."

"I'll talk to her. Do you know the other person?"

"No, I put the note on the dresser in the apartment, but I'll give you the name when I get back. You don't need it right now, do you? Because we plan on spending the weekend with Allison's family."

"It can wait."

They searched around for another hour. It was getting dark when the sheriff called it quits. "I'll get a search team out here tomorrow to see if they can find anything. Thanks for your help."

"You're always welcome."

After the sheriff left the area around ten-thirty, Chase, Allison, and her family sat around the fire, roasting marshmallows. The twins were sleeping in the cabin.

"What an afternoon," Ethan Winters said, sipping on his beer. "I've seen you twice, Chase, and both times it has involved the sheriff's department. Is this the life my daughter can look forward to?"

Allison interrupted her father. "Dad, enough. It's not Chase's fault these things happen."

"I'm not saying they are, Allison, but the point is they are happening, and I want to know how you feel about it."

Allison finished roasting her marshmallow. "I'm fine with it because I know Chase will never do anything to harm me or himself. He'll make sure I'm protected. That's important to me, and in the future, our family."

Haley's eyes widened. "You're pregnant."

Allison shook her head. "But someday we'll be married and have a family. I can't imagine having a family with anybody else."

Ethan glanced at Chase who just finished drinking his beer. "How do you feel about all of this?"

Chase set the empty can next to the log he sat on. "All of what Allison says will happen someday. She's right, there isn't anything I won't do to protect her or our children."

Garrett sighed. "I know how you feel. There isn't anything I wouldn't do for my wife and the twins."

Haley glared at her husband. "That's not necessarily true, because if you felt that way we wouldn't be discussing moving to a new job when you have a wonderful job in California."

Garrett frowned. "That's really not something we should be talking about with your father. It's a discussion between the two of us."

"Maybe you're right, Garrett, but don't say you'll do anything to take care of our family when you don't necessarily mean it." She climbed off the log and stormed to the cabin. Everyone was quiet around the campfire. Chase quickly changed the subject.

"Mr. Winters, what area of the state of Wyoming will you be traveling to next week?"

"To the Big Horn Mountains, west of Buffalo, in the higher elevations. It'll be a small project if it goes through, but of course there are major challenges. In this case, people don't want their hunting areas to be endangered, and I can't blame them."

Allison opened another beer and took a drink. "Dad, why are you part of this if you're behind the landowners?"

Her father eyed her as he chewed on his burnt marshmallow. "It's a job."

Haley returned and sat down next to her husband, taking his hand. "I'm sorry." She reached over and kissed him.

"It's okay," he said. "Are the kids okay?"

"Yeah, they're snuggled into each other fast asleep." Allison handed Haley a beer. Haley opened it and took a drink. "I still have the creeps that someone is watching us."

Chase slid down off the log and leaned back against it. "People have told me that they hear things and see things that aren't there a lot of times, but they still seem real. I asked them to explain it to me, but they couldn't. They just say the Rocky Mountains have their mysteries. I agree—these mountains are mystical."

Mr. Winters nodded. "I left ten years ago, and I've only been here a few months, but I can say that I've heard weird noises at night—noises which I can't explain. It's very mysterious. Chase, since you're a guy who enjoys mystery, this would be a perfect spot for you.”

They all turned at the howlings coming from the mountains. Chase doused the fire. “The wolves are telling us goodnight.”

Chapter 3

The next morning Allison and Haley prepared pancakes with bacon. Chase had taken the twins out to the lake to fish. Their father and Garrett sat outside, probably chatting about hunting and fishing. Allison joined her older sister at the stove.

"Are you okay?" asked Allison.

Haley flipped over some pancakes. "I'm better. Garrett and I talked some last night, and I told him I'd listen to what he had to say about the fishing and hunting job. I told him how I felt about changing jobs when he had such a good one, but he was right in saying that it just costs so much to live in California. Neither of us knows if Montana is the place for us either."

Allison lowered the temperature on the stove. "It's not fair for me to comment on any of what you're going through because of who I dated. Willis Shepherd had everything he wanted, and I could have had everything I wanted with him, but I never felt loved by him or his family. I feel love with Chase and his family." She used tongs to flip the bacon as they talked. "I didn't even know his family, but they took me in and made me feel like I was part of the family, and that was important to me. To be truthful, none of it would have mattered because I have feelings for Chase."

They looked up when the door opened and two young girls came running in with fish on a rope. "We each caught a fish," Melody said. "And they're big ones."

Haley knelt down to the girls. "They sure are. Did you tell Chase, thank you?"

"We sure did," Melanie said. "He showed us how to place the fish on the hook, toss the line into the water, then reel the fish in. It was hard to reel it in, but he was there to show us how to do it."

"I'm glad you had fun," Haley said. "Right now, it's time to get cleaned up because breakfast is ready."

After they ran into the bathroom to wash their hands, Allison peered over at Chase. "Thanks for taking the kids fishing."

"I enjoyed it. They have a lot of energy."

Allison placed bacon on the plate, and Chase put the plate on the table. He came back, wrapped his arm around her chest, and kissed her on the forehead. The door opened, and in walked her father and Garrett. "Just in time for breakfast," Allison said.

After breakfast, they walked the trails to see the sights. An eagle flew above them, deer grazed in the distance, and small birds and animals showed up unexpectedly. Chase stopped in his tracks and put his finger to his lips. Melody started to say something when her mother reached down and covered her hand over her mouth. Their eyes followed where Chase pointed.

He bent down next to the twins. "Don't move. Watch the black bear and see what he does."

They watched quietly as the bear reached into the creek and swiped out a fish. He sat on his back end and made a meal out of the fish. Moments later the bear finished his meal and lumbered back into the tree line.

"Wow, that was cool," Melody said.

Melanie added. "How did you know it was a he?"

Chase kept his eyes in that direction. "Because the bear was large and round. A female bear is much smaller."

Melody grinned. "How are you so smart?"

He winked. "I like to read."

After they finished their hike and ate lunch, they spent time in the lake swimming. All but Mr. Winters. That evening after dinner, they roasted marshmallows. The sun had set, and Chase and Allison were the only ones around the campfire.

Allison slipped between Chase's legs, and he wrapped his arms around her chest. "This was an enjoyable day," she said. "My nieces think a lot of you. Thank you for what you did for them today."

"I enjoyed everything also."

Allison held up her hand to admire her Montana sapphire ring in the moonlight. "We haven't talked about marriage, but you hinted at it when you gave me this ring."

"I've always planned on marrying you."

She peered up into his eyes. "Are you ever going to ask me?"

"Is that what you want?"

"I hope so." He shifted her onto his lap, took off her ring, then moved it to her right hand. He reached into his pocket, pulled out another small box, and opened it. Without a word, he placed the engagement ring on her left hand.

"Allison Taylor Winters, will you be my wife?"

Tears ran down her eyes.

"What's wrong?"

Allison's lips trembled. "Are you sure you want to marry someone who can't have children? I'm damaged goods."

He kissed her on the forehead. "Even if we never have a child, it won't change how I feel about you. You'll always be the only woman in my heart, so what about it? Will you be my wife?"

"Always and forever." She kissed him passionately then stopped. "I had better stop. This might not be the best place for such a thing."

"That's why there are blankets in the boat."

She kissed him once more. "Ah, you planned."

He carried her to the boat and laid her down in the middle of it. "This is perfect," Allison whispered.

Later, Chase pointed to the stars. "Many believe in making promises under the stars. My promise to you is I will do my best to love you."

"I knew that. I promise I'll always be in love with you, and I will let nothing ever come between us." She snuggled into him, and the rocking of the boat almost put her to sleep.

He whispered in her ear. "When do you want to get married?"

She shifted to peer into his eyes. "Would tomorrow be too soon?"

He chuckled. "Maybe give it a few days."

"How about August fifteenth? Your birthday is the tenth, mine is the twentieth."

"The fifteenth it is."

She rolled on top of him. "Now that's settled, let's continue with pressing needs."

Later that evening, Allison moved onto her back and stared at the star-filled sky. "This is amazing." Chase pulled the covers over them and pulled her close. "I feel like people are watching us," Allison said.

Chase gently stroked her hair. "Relax and try to sleep."

"Don't want to fall asleep. I don't want this night to end."

Chapter 4

Chase woke up when the sun started rising. He gazed at Allison whose face glowed as she slept. He was just as happy as she was about their future together. He lay there listening to the morning sounds of birds singing, water breaking gently against the boat, and the wind whispering in the trees. The choir calmed his spirit.

Her voice got his attention. "What's on your mind, dear?"

"I was thinking this boat might be a wonderful place to live. What do you think?"

She reached up and kissed him. "As long as I'm in your arms, I don't care where we live."

"You are so romantic."

She sat up, resting her head against his shoulder. "That's because I'm with the guy I'm in love with. We should get dressed because my dad is also an early riser."

The two ambled hand-in-hand to the cabin. Chase opened the door, and everything was quiet. "I'll put some coffee on," Chase said.

Allison touched his hand. "I'll start breakfast. How

does bacon and eggs sound?"

A few minutes later, Haley, still dressed in a robe, wiped the sleep from her eyes. She stopped and grinned at the two. "I'm sure it was pretty romantic sleeping in the boat."

Allison blushed. "How did you know?"

"You know I've always been a light sleeper. I heard the cabin door open or shut, plus I heard feet walking across the wooden floor."

Allison dropped eggs into the pan. "You figured it out. It was wonderful, and you're right—it's romantic sleeping on the boat. In fact, we may decide to buy a larger one, move on to it, and float around the lake."

Haley laughed. "Now that wouldn't surprise me."

They both turned to their father's voice. "What's so blasted funny? Don't you know I'm older, and I need my sleep?"

Haley rolled her eyes. "Sorry, Dad, but I was just joshing Allison about spending the night on the boat."

"Was it rocking to the waves?"

He and Haley laughed as Allison blushed. "You could say that. I do have some wonderful news," Allison said, holding out her left hand.

Haley grabbed it. "Wow, that is beautiful." She turned to Chase. "She's been waiting for you to ask her to marry her."

"And he did," Allison beamed. "Last night was the best night of my life."

They all turned when Garrett and the twins came into the kitchen. Melody stared at Allison. "You look different today. What's up?"

Haley picked up her little girl. "Uncle Chase has asked Aunt Allison to marry her."

Melanie rolled her eyes at Chase. "What took you so long?"

Everyone laughed. Allison changed the subject. "You all need to get washed up because breakfast is ready."

After breakfast and the hugs that followed, Chase and Allison climbed into the boat to head to the other end of the lake. Allison waved goodbye to her sister and her family. Once they were out of sight, she turned to Chase. "My dad didn't seem so happy about me getting married."

"Yeah, I noticed that. Does it bother you?"

She reached up and kissed him. "Nope, I don't care how my dad feels because I'm in love with you." She frowned. "There is something happening with my dad that I can't pinpoint." She shrugged. "Oh well, I'm not going to dwell on it. If he wants me to know what's going on, he'll tell me."

It was ten-thirty when they docked the boat, tied everything down, and drove to Mountain Ridge. They hadn't even been in the bookstore five minutes when the sheriff came strolling through. Chase grinned at him. "How was *your* weekend?"

Sheriff Portal laughed. "If you mean my Sunday, it was wonderful because I didn't have to chase down criminals. But now it's Monday, so that's what I'll be doing."

"How can we help?" Chase asked.

The sheriff rolled his eyes. "Glad you asked. I'm going to drive up to Whitefish today, and I would like you to join me to talk to the owner of the Whitefish Bar."

"Sure, I'll join you. Anything else?"

The sheriff eyed Allison. "Why do you look so different?"

Allison's face turned a beautiful shade of pink. "What do you mean?"

"You just look different."

She laughed. "If you mean I'm happy because Chase asked me to marry him, I am."

The sheriff hugged her. "Congratulations." He turned to Chase and shook his hand. "It's about time. When's the wedding?"

"August fifteenth," Allison smiled.

"I'll make sure to put that on my calendar. Are you ready to go?"

Chase nodded. "Let me grab a couple of things." He came back downstairs five minutes later. "I'm ready." He pulled Allison into his arms and kissed her. "I'll be back as soon as I can, future wifely one."

"Be safe, sweetheart and love of my life."

Chase and the sheriff climbed into the cruiser, heading north to Whitefish. "You two do make a cute couple. You're good for her as she is for you. What made you decide it was time?"

"I had always planned on asking her to marry me, and this past weekend was the perfect opportunity, so I did. Enough about that, what do you hope to find out from the lady in Whitefish?"

"The bartender? She's the one who gave you the paper? She has tons of information about everything, but it usually takes something to entice her to open up."

"Money?"

The sheriff huffed and shook his head. "Exactly. I plan on offering a reward for information leading to any information associated with the young gal in the hospital. Her leg was broken in three different places, but she's still breathing, and the doctor is hopeful she'll survive. She still hasn't woken up, so we haven't been able to identify who she is."

They arrived in Whitefish around noon, parked in front of the bar, and walked in. A woman with graying blond hair washed glasses behind the bar.

She glanced up when the bell over the door rang. "Sheriff Portal, what brings you here today? You brought that handsome man I met once before. I bet you want to know about the young woman who was hurt badly."

Sheriff Portal chuckled. "I might have known rumors would run rampant around the county."

Leah laughed. "The woman's name is Myra Kent, and her boyfriend is Chester Mueller."

"And how would you know that?" the sheriff asked.

She handed him a piece of paper. He stared at the names on the paper "What is this?"

Leah wiped down the top of the bar. "All the names of those who participated in the most recent mystery hunt."

"Why would you have this?"

She finished and flung the rag in the sink. "Simple, I'm one of the stops for those who are on the mystery hunt. What I mean by that is this is where they pick up the participants and drop them off when the hunt ends."

"So, you know what happens up there?"

She shook her head as she grabbed a clean rag and washed out a glass. "Nope. Someone else knows that."

"Would you know who that someone would be?"

"Nope," she said once more. "Each part of the mystery hunt is kept separate."

Chase interrupted. "Sheriff, may I ask a question?" When he nodded, Chase studied Leah. "If they stopped before and after, wouldn't anyone have noticed that two people were missing?"

She shrugged. "It would make sense, except when they come back down, it's like they don't know what happened at all during the weekend."

Chase's eyes widened. "Are you saying some kind of mind-altering drug is used?"

"I don't know what to tell you other than they stop by here before and after, and that's all I know."

The sheriff jumped in. "Why are you part of this?"

Leah laughed. "Money of course. Everyone comes to this bar. Plus, the organizers purchase a keg or two here for the weekend."

As they drove back to Mountain Ridge, the sheriff was silent. "What are you trying to figure out?" Chase asked.

The sheriff stared straight ahead when he spoke. "How did Leah get the names of those people? I ran the names on the list after you nodded off, and most of those names are known troublemakers who just haven't been caught. However, the one who was killed and the young lady who is struggling to survive have never had problems with the law—at least their fingerprints aren't in the system. I'm going to talk to each one of the participants this week."

Silence ensued on their trip back until the sheriff glanced his way. "Can you see what you can find out about that area in your books, and see if the books have any more info about the names of those associated with the mystery hunt?"

"I can do that."

Sheriff Portal sighed. "I'm sure you're wondering why I involve you with all this and not my deputies. First of all, we've worked well together and have been able to solve mysteries that have been hampering the county for many years. More importantly, I trust you, and right now I can't trust those in the department."

"Because of what Gartner and Shepherd's lawyers said about your deputies being incompetent and corrupt?"

The sheriff nodded.

Chase exhaled. "You've been associated with criminals for many years, and you realize how manipulative they can be. Maybe that's what's happening here."

"I don't agree. There's some truth to what the hot-shot attorneys are saying. The problem is they lumped all the deputies into the same category, but I don't believe that's true. The only corrupt deputy was the one who worked with Gartner."

"Then what's the problem?"

"When the public finds out one is corrupt, they believe that we're all corrupt, and even though it's not true, it's hard to get rid of that stigma. It's tough enough for law enforcement the way it is. We don't need this kind of crap, so I've been thinking about how we can clean up our act and bring the public back on our side."

"In two words, public relations," Chase said. "For instance, increase patrols during certain holidays and events. Maybe hold events for the community. I'm sure you do some of those things already."

"We do. For instance, on the Fourth of July we increased security, which turned out to be a positive. You're right, we need to continue doing those sorts of things, and we will. Right now, I'm going to have a conversation with the ladies and gentlemen on the list, and if you would be so kind, see if you can find some sort of connection with your books and computer. Of course, after you say hello to your fiancée."

Chapter 5

"Do you think you can actually find anything out about these people?" Allison nestled into the crook of his arm in their bed.

"I don't know but I'll see what I can do. Hopefully I can find something out about them."

"I have confidence in my sweetheart." She sat up quickly. "What if we could find a way to be involved in the upcoming mystery hunt?"

He frowned at her. "Would you want to do that?"

"Not necessarily, but I did enjoy our time in the Bernard house searching for gold, despite all the craziness."

He kissed her on the forehead. "I didn't know my fiancée was so adventurous."

She kissed him back and grinned. "I do like to explore." She buried herself under the blankets.

Chase took a deep breath. "I would say you do."

The next morning Allison had just opened the bookstore when her father walked in. "Good morning, Dad."

"Good morning. I stopped by to tell you goodbye."

Allison's eyes went wide. "What are you saying?"

He let out a breath. "I'm going back to California with your sister and her family. I wasn't cut out to do this type of work, and Haley said I could stay with her."

Allison scowled. "You're back to using drugs again. I thought you had kicked it."

"It's not that easy. Garrett knows of a rehab center that can help. I just wanted to tell you goodbye and good luck in the future."

Allison hugged him. "I would have helped you."

"You have no space for me here."

"We have an extra bedroom you could have slept in."

"I'd rather be in California. Besides, this relationship won't last for you."

Allison didn't know what to say. She released him and stepped back.

"What do you mean it won't last?"

He took a deep breath. "You're a Winters, and Winters are never satisfied for long. They always jump in and out of relationships. You've done it twice before."

She grimaced. "You're wrong, Dad. Chase is the one I'll be with forever."

He stared at her, then lifted her chin with his finger. "This is goodbye."

Allison wiped a tear off her cheek. "I hope you find some happiness in your life."

He smiled. "I hope you do too."

"You don't understand, I've found the man I've been looking for all my life." She watched as her father walked out the door, knowing she possibly would never see him again.

"Is everything okay?" She turned and buried her

head on Chase's shoulder.

"I don't know if I'll see my father again."

Chase stroked her hair. "I'm sorry."

She lifted her head up to see his face. "Promise you'll never leave me?"

"I'm not going anywhere."

She took his hands, and they sat on the edge of the desk. "It shouldn't surprise me. Our family has the habit of running away. I did the same thing when I was sixteen."

He lifted her head up so he could see her eyes. "You were escaping a horrible situation."

She frowned. "I still left, and I'm afraid I will again. That's just who the family is. My dad was right."

They both turned when the door opened, and an older man walked in with a smile. "I'm looking for westerns."

~

The Fourth of July celebration arrived in Mountain Ridge. It consisted of a parade, kids' events, and a softball tournament. In addition, all the emergency crews had stations for citizens to check out along Main Street. That night there would be a street dance, and the celebration would conclude with a fireworks display.

Chase kept the two stores open throughout the day. Allison, with help from the high school students who worked there, set up a couple patriotic displays on Main Street.

For the event Allison dressed up in a sequined stars-and-stripes dress, while Xavier's girlfriend, Anastasia, was in a Betsy Ross colonial ladies' costume. Chase and Xavier dressed as Uncle Sam.

Allison and Anastasia manned a table outside the

stores that displayed books and antiques related to the Fourth of July. Milo and his wife, dressed up as a cowboy and cowgirl, ambled up to the display table.

Allison grinned. "Who is this?"

Milo smiled. "We're just a couple of cowpokes."

"You two look perfect."

"As you two do," Milo's wife said.

The four chatted for a bit before they moved on. The hours lingered slowly as people stopped to look at the display. Chase and Xavier joined them to help them put everything back in the stores as the day came to an end. Once completed, the two teenagers were on their merry way.

"They make a cute couple, as do we," Allison said. "Let's go grab something to eat."

They headed toward the smell of fried onions that emanated from the center square, and bought greasy hamburgers, then found a table to sit at. Several moments later Glen Allan and Penelope joined them.

"You two are dressed in the holiday spirit," Glen Allan said.

"It's a first for me," Chase said. "Allison looks beautiful, so I didn't want to be the oddball."

Glen Allan laughed. "She does look nice, but then she always has."

Chase stood up and threw away their paper wrappers. "I need to take care of some things at the bookstore." He waved and headed toward the store.

Everyone switched their glance toward a stylish woman who walked toward them, wearing a jacket, pair of blue jeans, and ankle boots.

"Oh my gosh, it's really you, Sophia?" Allison said, hugging her best friend.

She smiled. "I told you I would be coming to Montana."

Allison sighed. "I've been so busy with everything else that I must have forgotten about it."

Sophia turned to the other woman. "Penelope, how have you been?"

Penelope smiled. "Well. Work has been stressful because it's been so busy, but Allison is the one we should be talking about. What do you have on your finger?"

Allison smiled. "I gladly accepted Chase's marriage proposal."

The others congratulated her. "When is this going to happen?" Penelope asked.

"August fifteenth," Allison smiled. "And I can't wait."

Sophia eyed Allison. "I'm happy for you. Where is the man you're going to marry?"

"He had to take care of some things in the bookstore and antique store," Glen Allan said. "Even during a holiday celebration, the man is still working."

They turned to Chase's voice. "I'm glad I hurried back to the store. There was actually an old man getting ready to lift a book." He stopped and gazed at Sophia. "Wow, you look so different. What did you do to yourself?"

Sophia blushed. "I dyed my hair a light brown and cut it into a shaggy look as a step to change my outlook in life. It's good to see you again."

The two hugged each other. Sophia stepped back quickly. "What happened to the book thief?"

Chase grinned. "I gave him the book since he said he'd been searching for it for a couple of years."

Glen Allan laughed. "Chase Connor, you've always been so gullible."

Over the next hour they ate too much and chatted. Sophia had just finished a bite of her hot dog when she turned to Allison. "How long have you two been engaged?"

Allison smiled. "He asked me a week ago while we were at my dad's cabin on Smith Lake. I had hoped he would ask me, and he did. I can't wait."

Glen Allan interrupted. "How are you and Kirby doing?"

Sophia didn't answer at first. "We're doing okay. He didn't join me since he had a big deal happening in Boston that he had to finish this week."

"I'm sorry to hear that," Penelope said. "You two make such a wonderful couple."

Sophia's eyes darted to Chase, then to Penelope. "Thanks. What is it with you and Glen Allan? Late nights?"

Everyone laughed. Glen Allan explained. "It's not that way. We both have set boundaries with each other regarding work, boundaries that we both can live with. We don't spend a minute past nine in the office."

Chase laughed. "You just finish the rest at your condo."

Glen Allan smirked. "You know me so well, Chase Connor." He sipped on his beer, then turned to Sophia. "I'm sure you're aware of what's happening with your father and brother?"

She nodded. "Mom has brought me up to date. It seems like they were roped into the situation, at least that's what my mother said."

"And you believe her?" Allison asked.

Sophia frowned. "I don't know all that happened, so why wouldn't I?"

Allison's face warmed. "You realize they were going to murder Chase for his money."

Sophia took a deep breath, then shifted toward Chase. "I'm sorry about that, Chase."

"How could you have known?"

Allison was ready to say something else when Chase put his finger to her lips. "It's the Fourth of July. Forget about all that, and let's enjoy ourselves."

"I agree," Glen Allan said. "I'm sorry I brought the whole situation up."

After eating their dinner, Chase and Allison strolled down the street checking the different booths. "Let's grab a pie," Allison said.

They walked over and purchased a piece of apple pie. The proceeds went to a local church that fed and housed the less fortunate. As they walked, they enjoyed their pie.

When they passed a booth called the Mystery Hunt, Chase stopped. "Do you think that is what the sheriff is talking about?'

Allison had just finished her last bite of pie. "Let's find out." She took the paper plate and dumped it into one of the many garbage cans on Main Street. They stood behind a couple of people in line before they made it to the front.

A man with a nametag that read Brink smiled up at them. "Are you two ready for another adventure?"

Chase's expression didn't change. "You're part of this?"

"Yes, I am and have been for the last couple of years. Are you signing up?"

Chase let out his breath. "First explain to us what this is all about."

"It's a weekend getaway in the highest part of Flathead County. There's fishing, hiking, campfire activities, and much more."

Allison brushed a piece of hair out of her eye. "It's a weekend to unwind?"

Brink grinned. "That's a great way to put it."

Chase let a breath out. "How do we sign up?"

Brink handed him some paperwork. "Fill these out. The cost is five hundred dollars for the weekend."

"Perfect birthday present for us, dear," Allison said.

After Chase filled out the paperwork, he gave Brink a debit card. Brink swiped it, then gave it back with a receipt. "Here is the pickup point at Smith Lake."

"You don't pick up at the bar in Whitefish?" Chase asked.

"We rotate where we pick up people."

"Sounds good. Will you be there?"

Brink shook his head. "I just sign them up. Hope you enjoy it."

Allison had one last question. "How safe is it?"

"There are security guards up there that watch over everything. Why do you ask?"

"We heard about the woman who fell off the mountain and broke her leg."

"That was a sad situation. She and her boyfriend were into heavy drugs. The morning of the accident, they decided they'd had enough and ran away. Security tried to get to them, but it was too late. They both had fallen."

Chase frowned. "Why didn't security make others aware?"

Brink's face changed. "The event takes place on private property, and there is no communication allowed up there for the weekend. If you don't have any other questions, I have others who are waiting to sign up."

Chase and Allison left. "Strange the way he acted about the security issue," Allison mentioned.

"And the changing venue," Chase added. "I'll pass it on to the sheriff. Either Brink or Leah could be lying. Leah is the woman who runs the bar in Whitefish, where she told the sheriff that the participants are picked up and dropped off. But you're right, strange happenings all the way around." Chase took her hand. "Should we go find a spot to park for the fireworks?"

She batted her eyes. "I have the perfect spot, so we can have our own fireworks afterward."

Chapter 6

The next day a young guy with red hair and braces walked into the bookstore. "Can I help you?" Chase asked.

The guy wiped the sweat off his face. "Are you the book mystery guy?"

Chase's eyes widened. "What do you mean?"

"I heard there's a guy in Mountain Ridge who reads books and is able to solve mysteries from reading the book."

"I've helped the sheriff at times solve mysteries with the help of a book I've read, if that's what you're asking?"

"Do you believe in ghosts?"

Without thinking, Chase took a step back, not sure what to say. "I believe there are things out there that are hard to fathom. Maybe you can explain a little bit more about what you're looking for. How about I get you a soda or a cup of coffee?"

"A soda would be great."

"I'll be right back." He came out with two sodas and handed the young man one Immediately he opened the soda and drank almost the whole can in one gulp. "I was thirsty."

"I can tell. Where are you from?"

"I live near Creston on a homestead with my mother. My father died several years ago, and my sister has since left. If you drew a triangle, you'd land on Creston, Mount Aeneas, and Echo Lake at its points. In that triangle of land, the strangest things are happening. For instance, when you go near Echo Lake, you hear murmuring off the lake—a young girl calling for help. There's talk that at a certain spot at Mount Aeneas, people have heard voices through the passes, language that no one has heard before."

"Interesting. Have you heard any of this?"

The guy met his eyes. "Yes, I have. I enjoy traveling to Mount Aeneas to watch the sunset and think about where my life is going. Although I want to move forward, I have to take care of my mom because she is handicapped and has no one to watch over her."

Chase grabbed a piece of paper. "I can check it out. What is your name?"

"It's Sylvester Coon. Are you Chase Connor?"

"I am."

Sylvester took a deep breath. "I had hoped you were. Most the people I talk to think I'm hearing things, that I'm on crack or something. I do not do drugs."

"Sometimes people act that way when they can't understand what's happening. Don't let it bother you. I'll help you figure this out. What do you want to know?"

He drained the last swallow of his soda. "I want to know if I'm weirding out, or if there's something actually out there. At the least, I'd like to know if someone else hears those noises like I do."

"I can understand. Write down as much information as you can about what you've heard, and I'll check it out. Be as specific as you can be about the words you heard. Also, provide me information about anyone else who I could talk to who's also heard things."

"Like I said, Mr. Connor, the voices in the mountain I couldn't understand, so it makes me believe it's Native American."

"Do the best you can. What do you do for a living?"

"I work in Columbia Falls at the local bar as a bartender."

"And is your mother retired?"

Sylvester shook his head. "As I said she's handicapped, and she has a hard time getting around. One of her friends lives with us and helps take care of her, so it works out."

"Do you have anything else you can tell me?" Chase could tell Sylvester's mind was working by the frown on his face. "I know there's a Montana Historical Society Guide that has a bit of information about the area, but I don't know what the name of the book is."

"I can check that out. What about historians or experts in the area?"

Again, Sylvester thought. "There is an older Native American who lives near Echo Lake who may be able to help you. I think his name is Edgar Blacktail or something like that. He has a cabin and a big dog, and he won't let anyone near him."

"That's something to work with."

Sylvester checked his watch. "I have to get to work. I hope you find something or at least find out that

I'm not going nuts."

"I'm sure that's not the case. If others hear voices or noises, there is something happening out there."

He glanced at Chase. "Do *you* think I'm out of it?"

Chase ran his fingers through his hair. "Since I've been in Montana, I've run into three men who could be considered Bigfoots, found a million-dollar treasure, and found photos of young girls buried in the ground, so no I don't think you're nuts. There is something out there and I'll find it."

"Thanks."

After he shut the door, Allison's voice sounded behind him. "What did you get yourself into now, my dear love?"

"Just helping a young man who is hearing voices."

After dinner, Chase and Allison strolled down to the Mountain Ridge Bar & Grill. They frequented the place every so often to grab a drink, dance, and hear whatever gossip Jake, the owner, had to tell them. Allison linked onto Chase's arm as they walked. "The last time we were down here was when you and I first hooked up together."

"That's true. Tonight is different."

She rolled her eyes. "You're on an information hunt with the local gossip."

"Maybe Jake has heard things about that area. At least it's worth a try."

She kissed him on the cheek. "If nothing else I get to spend time with my favorite guy."

Chase opened the door for Allison who headed toward the bar. They found two seats in the corner and sat down. Jake hurried over to them. "Wow, who do we have here? Let's see the ring, Allison." He laughed at her surprised face. "Come on Allison, I know everything that happens around here. Your dad told me you were engaged to the 'mystery book guy' before he left."

"That's what he said?" Chase asked.

"Exact words," Jake said. "He didn't seem to be happy that his youngest daughter was marrying some guy who reads and sells books for a living. Think he preferred a guy with money, but I couldn't tell him that Chase here is richer than most people in the county as a whole."

"I appreciate it," Chase said.

"A couple of beers?"

"Wonderful," Allison said.

Chase's eyes scanned around the bar and grill and landed on Willis who was with a gal he had never seen before. "Who is Willis with? And why is he even out of jail?"

Allison turned to see where Chase was looking. "That's Debbie Grant. He used to date her before he and I hooked up. The second question I can't answer."

Jake handed them two beers. "I can answer the second question. The judge released the Shepherd family on bail because of their long-standing work with Flathead County. I also understand that Gartner waived extradition and is on his way to California to face federal charges in that state."

Allison finished sampling her beer. "Why would he do something like that?"

Chase shrugged. "For several reasons. One could mean reduced jail time; another would allow him to address the charges sooner. In addition, the legal system may show favor for his willingness to cooperate with the judicial system. It could lead to a plea deal. There are other benefits, but those may be the main ones."

Allison's eyes widened. "Does that mean Gartner may not spend any time in jail?"

"There's always that possibility in any criminal case."

"Wow," Allison said.

Chase changed the subject. "Jake, have you heard of a triangle of sorts that would include Creston, Mount Aeneas, and Echo Lake?"

"What are you talking about?"

Chase grabbed a napkin, drew points for the three areas, then finished by drawing a triangle connecting the three points. "A young man came into the bookstore today to have me research some eerie happenings in that area. For instance, he and others have heard voices throughout the mountains and echoes around the lake."

The bartender leaned his elbows on the bar. "I heard a story about a chief named Aeneas leading the Kootenai over Maria Pass on snowshoes in the 1860s. I'm not sure why but I would guess he was trying to escape the cavalry."

Jake pointed to the other end of the bar when two customers stood waiting. Once he provided them with their drinks, he hurried back to Chase and Allison. "Some ranchers told me about some strange happenings on the flatland in that area. One lost several cattle, but those who checked into it thought it was either wolves or coyotes. The strange thing is they didn't find any carcasses."

Allison jumped in. "The cattle could have been stolen?"

"Possible, but nobody knows. The sheriff's

department chalked it up to predators who dragged the cattle to another location, which they never found." Jake laughed. "Are you now the go-to man for mysterious or strange phenomena in the area?"

"I enjoy figuring out things like this. There has to be a reason why these things happen, but most people don't take the time to figure them out, so now that I have a wonderful bookstore manager, I can do some research."

Allison's face lit up. "Aw, that's so sweet you would say something like that. However, I told you I'm going with you, since every time you go out on your own, something happens to you. Now if something happens, it will be to both of us."

"Keep me posted, I have to get to work," Jake said. "If I hear anything, I'll let you know."

Chapter 7

Early the next morning Chase and Allison drove east toward Creston. The ride was quiet except for the news on the radio. Allison entertained herself peering out the side window for wild animals. Finally, Chase broke the silence. "So, you knew Sophia was coming back to Montana?"

She nodded. "I was so excited about our engagement I just didn't think much about it. Does it bother you?"

Chase shook his head. "I'm marrying you, but she needs you."

Allison glanced at him. "That's one of the reasons I love you. You care about others. I'll talk to her when we get back."

As they approached Creston, Allison googled anything she could find about the town. "Creston soil is considered some of the most fertile in the state. We should visit the Creston Center," Allison said. "It is home to the Creston Fish and Wildlife Center, as well as the Swan River National Wildlife Refuge."

"I take it the Creston Center deals specifically with the agriculture needs of the Flathead Valley," Chase said.

"Correct. According to its website, 'its primary purpose is to conduct research aimed at improving agricultural production and finding innovative solutions to problems faced by local producers.' They do crop trials, pest management, and soil health studies." She googled some more. "There are several other businesses located in Creston— a couple of construction companies and a realtor business."

They traveled through Creston, then continued toward Mount Aeneas. As they moved toward the mountain, Allison did some more searching on google and found out that Chief Aeneas, who the mountain was named for, played a significant role in guiding the Kootenai people during the challenges of European settlement.

"Listen to this, Chase, Chief Aeneas led the Kootenai over the mountains, just like Jake said."

"Interesting. Maybe that's who Sylvester and others hear. Does it give reasons why they went over the mountain?"

"The article says, 'Preservation of culture, access to resources, and strategic relocation. The terrain provided a natural barrier against further encroachment and offered a defensible position.' They also found water, shelter, and hunting grounds."

They arrived at the mountain around ten-thirty. Chase pulled into an area where others had parked and shut off the Jeep. "Are you ready to go for a hike?"

"I brought plenty of bug spray because I do know there are a lot of bugs and bees along the trails."

They started their trek up a fairly steep incline and stopped about thirty minutes into it. "This is a challenging hike," Chase said. "Imagine what the Native Americans went through back in the 1860s."

Allison pointed to a ledge above them. "Mountain goats." She pulled out her cell phone and took several photos. "Amazing."

Chase put his finger to his mouth. What had he heard? When she started to ask, he whispered, "Listen."

They both stood still for a few moments and Allison's mouth dropped. "I heard voices. I don't know Native American languages, but it sure sounded like that. Did you hear it?"

"I did. Maybe we should have paid a visit to Edgar Blacktail who lives near Echo Lake before we came up here. Let's finish the hike, and we'll make our way back to him."

An hour later they reached the summit and found a rock to sit on to view the scenery. Allison climbed on Chase's lap, wrapped her arms around his neck, and they searched the area. "This is gorgeous," she said. "I've lived here for several years, and I've never seen anything like this." She pointed to an eagle flying above them.

Chase pointed to what was probably a bear further away down the mountain. They sat quietly for the next thirty minutes listening to the sounds of nature. It was early afternoon when they headed down the mountain, arriving back at the Jeep an hour later. They climbed into the vehicle and drove toward Echo Lake.

"What do you think?" Allison asked.

"I heard many natural sounds of animals, birds, the wind, but there were also some unnatural sounds I couldn't identify. How about you?"

"The same. And I truly thought I heard voices, not

only foreign voices, but English voices also. Could it be that the English voices I heard were the Cavalry searching for the Kootenai?"

Chase drove out of the parking lot and onto the road. "It's hard to believe what we heard was anything other than just the sounds of the mountains."

"Sweetheart, we both heard more than that. If I hadn't heard it, I wouldn't have believed it myself, but we did hear something more than just the wind in the mountains. Maybe this Edgar Blacktail can add more to it."

An hour later they found a small cabin just outside of Echo Lake, the landscape of the cabin festooned with different Native American statues. The cabin needed a roof job, as well as work on the outside of the cabin. They parked the Jeep and climbed out of the vehicle.

"Did I say you could come onto my property?"

Allison huddled behind Chase and held onto his shoulders.

Chase nodded at the Native American. "You must be Edgar Blacktail."

"Who's asking?"

"My name is Chase Connor, and behind me is my fiancée, Allison Winters. A young man approached us about checking out some mysteries in the local area."

"You must be talking about what some people say is a triangle that includes Creston, the mountain, and the lake."

"We are. I run a bookstore, and I understand you're into Native American lore."

The older man twirled his long braid. "You're Chase Connor, the mystery book man?"

Chase laughed. "That's the second time I've heard

that. I love to read books, I learn things from books, and another way I learn things is talking to people. That's why we're here."

The old man twirled his hair once more, staring at them. "Come on in and we can talk."

Chase and Allison followed him into the cabin. The walls were covered with Native American beadwork, pottery, and woven textiles.

"Please join me around the central hearth or what you would call a fireplace. The Kootenai consider this a focal point providing warmth and a place for cooking. It is also a gathering spot for storytelling and communal activities. Please have a seat."

Just as Allison sat down, an old German shepherd came lumbering up and started licking Allison's face. "Koi, please leave the young woman alone."

"It's okay," Allison said. "I love dogs."

The German shepherd lay down next to Allison.

Edgar carried a tray with three drinks of red juice for them. "This is a chokecherry juice. We enjoy the drink, and it reflects the understanding and respect for the natural world around us." He joined them. "Ask me what you want to know about the triangle."

Chase tasted his berry juice and set the glass down. "This is very good. We just started our research with a trek up the six-mile trail at the mountain. While there, we spent most of the day listening to different nature sounds that included the wind, but we also thought we heard voices in English and what could be Native American." He took another sip. "We had heard and read about the Kootenai chief who led his tribe over the mountain to find a better way of life. Tell me, have you heard these sounds yourself?"

Edgar put his glass down and lifted a shoulder. "People do report hearing voices in the mountains, but the phenomenon could be attributed to several factors, mostly relating to echoes. Mountains can create acoustic effects, causing sounds to echo, and sometimes making it seem like voices come from different directions." His eyes lit on Chase. "What do you want from me?"

Chase met his gaze. "Neither one of us can speak your tongue so we wondered if you would join us on the mountain, just listen, and tell us what you hear."

He stood up. "We still have plenty of time to get there before darkness falls. That is when we will hear more than during the day. Be prepared for what you hear."

Chapter 8

Chase drove the Jeep toward the mountain once more, arriving as the sun started to set. They parked the Jeep, climbed out, and started up the trail.

Edgar stopped at an open spot. "We should gather branches, whatever we can find. It will be cold after dark." They did that and a few minutes later had a fire going. "While we wait, I'll give you a history lesson." He pulled a bottle of whiskey out of his bag. "And also drink."

They sat on one side of the fire, facing one of the trails leading into the mountains. After taking a swig of whiskey, Edgar started. "No one knows exactly which trail my people took over the mountain, but many believe the most logical spot is that trail," he said pointing. "It was a strenuous trail, but Chief Aeneas felt it would be difficult for the soldiers to find."

He took another drink, and this time passed it to Chase who wiped the top off and took a drink. He handed it to Allison who shook her head. Once Edgar had reclaimed the bottle, he started once more.

"It is said the soldiers searched for several days but couldn't find the Kootenai and finally gave up. My people could breathe for a little while.

Chase put his fingers to his lips. They all listened to the sounds. Edgar's eyes widened.

"Do you hear that?" he said.

"Yes," Chase said. "I hear different voices—male voices, English and foreign."

Edgar smiled. "The Kootenai have lost the soldiers, and the soldiers are frustrated because their scouts have lost the trail, but then the Native Americans are good at that sort of thing. My people are talking at the top of the mountain, wondering whether they should fire on them or not. One warrior says 'no,' and then the voices go away."

They listened for several more minutes and didn't hear anymore.

"They are gone now," Edgar said. "We should go."

As they climbed down the mountain, Allison finally spoke, "I understood plainly what the soldiers were saying, but I wouldn't have believed it if I didn't hear it. You sure it wasn't just the mountain?"

Edgar stopped and glanced at Allison. "Most people just believe the sounds are the winds and the other noises in the mountains, but if you listen closely, you will hear other things. That is what happened tonight. You will never forget what you heard, and it will make you think differently once you come to these mountains again."

Allison sighed. "I wasn't scared or anything like that, but it was kind of eerie hearing those voices."

They climbed into the Jeep, and Chase drove them back to Edgar's cabin. Once there, Edgar turned to Chase. "You are welcome to spend the night in my cabin and then make your way back to the city in the morning."

"Thank you," Chase said.

Once they were in the cabin, Edgar grabbed them a warm blanket. "I'm sorry I don't have another bed. The floor is all I have for you to sleep on."

"It's okay," Chase said. "We'll make do on the floor with the blanket. I'm sure we'll be fine."

"It is a bear skin blanket from a grizzly I killed one day up there several years ago."

After Edgar left the room, Allison made a spot for her and Chase near the center of the room but not too close to the fireplace. After they shed their shoes and crawled under the blanket, Allison snuggled into Chase's arms.

"What a night," he said, kissing her on the forehead. "It was amazing being able to understand what they were saying, if that's what they were saying. Maybe it's all a hoax. It could be, but we'll never know. I've always thought that there are strange phenomena out there that no one can explain."

Allison shifted her body. "You've said that, and I don't disagree with that, but it's still hard to comprehend that there are actually voices out there from hundreds of years ago, and it's not the mountain playing tricks on the mind."

"No matter how you look at it, tonight was an amazing evening."

She kissed him. "It was, and it's too bad we can't continue this amazing evening, but I can't in someone else's house, so I'm going to call it a night." Allison buried her head in Chase's chest and within minutes was snoring lightly.

Chase lay awake thinking about what Edgar said

they had heard. The only thing that came out of this trip was the fact that Sylvester was not crazy. The three of them had heard voices also.

Tomorrow they'd head to Echo Lake. Deep down Chase believed there was more to the story than a woman's cry; there was something mysterious going on. It could be that the woman was crying out for help, or maybe it was something more nefarious. That was his last thought as he drifted off to sleep.

The next morning Chase opened his eyes to see Edgar standing near the stove, his back to Chase.

"I see you are awake. Good morning."

Chase grinned. "Now you have eyes behind your head?"

Edgar turned around with a light laugh. "You could say that. Wake your loved one up. Breakfast is almost ready."

Chase gently ran his fingers down her spine. Allison's eyes popped open quickly. "Is everything okay?"

"It is. Almost time for breakfast."

She lifted her head and kissed him. "Good morning, sweetheart. I slept so well last night in your arms."

"Good morning to you, too."

Allison sat up and turned toward where Edgar was cooking. "That smells wonderful."

"I hope you like it. It's ready."

Once they were out of the blanket, they folded it up and laid it in a corner.

"You can wash up over there," Edgar said, pointing to a wash basin.

Once they completed that task, they joined him at

the table. Sitting in front of them was some kind of bread with different types of jellies on the table.

"This is called bannock, which is a type of bread made from flour, baking powder, and in this case sugar. I fried it, and you can put honey or one of the different types of jam on it."

"It looks good," Allison said.

While they were eating, Chase brought up the woman's voice at Echo Lake.

"I have heard the voice," Edgar said. "The woman needs help. I've searched several times but have not been able to locate where the voice is coming from. You will check yourself?"

"We plan on it."

"After breakfast, I will show you where I heard the noise. We can go from there."

"Will you help?" Allison asked.

Edgar finished his last bite of bread. "Sure will. I look forward to working with the book man who seems to be able to solve these mysteries."

Chapter 9

Once they'd cleaned up the breakfast dishes, they climbed in the Jeep, and Chase drove toward Echo Lake.

It was only a ten-minute drive to one of the public lake access areas. After Chase found a parking spot, they exited the vehicle.

"Montana lakes are so beautiful," Allison said, taking in the scenery.

"That's why I stay here," Edgar said. "I'll take you to the place where I heard the sounds."

They walked along the edge of the lake until they came upon a path.

"I was fishing right there." Edgar shifted his weight to point at the trail. "The sound came from up there."

Chase jumped in. "Do you remember what was said?"

"Help me."

Chase took a deep breath. "Should we take a look?"

"That's why we're here," Edgar said.

Chase started toward the trail. Allison grabbed his hand and walked beside him with Edgar following.

Several minutes later they reached the end of the path which happened to be the top of the hill. They stood there eyeing the rocks and trees around them. Allison squeezed Chase's hand. "This is magnificent."

"It is," Chase said. "Let's look around to see if we can hear the voice and maybe determine what direction it comes for."

For the next thirty minutes, they searched in different directions but couldn't find anything. Edgar stood there scratching his beard. "Not a thing."

"We should get back to Mountain Ridge, and I'll do some research in the books to see if there is anything related to voices in this area."

They hiked back to the Jeep, and they dropped Edgar off at his cabin, then drove toward home. Both were quiet on the drive back. Once they arrived at the back of the bookstore, Chase turned off the Jeep and turned to Allison. "What did you think about the last twenty-four hours?"

"I don't know what to think other than I enjoyed spending it with you. Plus, I'm hungry."

"Let's grab something at the bar and grill."

"I like that idea."

They walked the three blocks to the bar. Once they stepped in to the crowded place, Chase found the only available table in the corner, and they hurried over to claim it.

The waitress joined them several minutes later. "Chase, Allison, it's good to see you."

"How have you been, Anastasia?" Allison asked.

"Wonderful. Just found out I was accepted at the University of Montana. Xavier did also."

"I'm happy for the two of you," Allison said.

"The special today is spaghetti and meatballs."

"I'll have that with water," Allison said.

"Same here," Chase said.

Once she left, Chase wrapped his arm around Allison's shoulders.

She snuggled in. "I had a wonderful day, but every day I'm with you is wonderful."

Chase chuckled. "It's safe to say it's eventful."

She lifted her eyes to his. "Eventful is a good word, but it can also mean dangerous."

Ten minutes later, Jake brought their meal. "How's my favorite couple?"

"We're doing well," Chase said.

"Good for you two. Enjoy the meal."

After finishing their dinner, they climbed into the Jeep. Allison took his hand. "How 'bout we take a ride in my new boat?"

"Sounds like a good idea."

Chase drove ten minutes to where their boat was anchored. Once out of the car, they headed toward the boat attached to a rented dock. He started the engine while Allison unwrapped the ropes holding it to the dock. She jumped into the boat, and they sped off onto the lake.

"Where to?" Chase asked.

"Nowhere in particular. I just wanted to get away from everything for an hour or so."

They sped toward the middle of the lake where Chase dropped the anchor. "This is a good place to watch the sun set," he said.

Allison grabbed a couple of beers out of the stocked chest and sat down next to Chase on a front bench.

"It was a good idea to keep the chest full," she said as she cracked open a beer and handed it to him.

After she opened hers and took a swig, she took Chase's hand. "Why did you decide to buy a boat?"

He smirked. "You mean why did I buy an old boat that needs work?"

She laughed. "I never thought of that, but let's go with that."

He wrapped his arm around her. "I don't know other than I do like the water, which is weird since I'm not a very good swimmer."

She reached up to kiss him. "It's a good thing we have life preservers."

They both listened to the waves gently hitting the boat. "Buying this boat is another way for me to find some peace in my life."

She tasted her beer. "Was it so bad in your family? They were so nice to me."

"It wasn't necessarily that they were bad; it was more of what was expected of me. I didn't know if I wanted to be a lawyer, but everyone in the family was a lawyer so it was expected of me." He took a swallow of his drink. "Now my brothers and sister want me to take over the law firm. My dad is currently the senior partner, but my grandfather wrote in his will that I must make partner at the first of the year."

"And you're not going to do it?"

He peered into her eyes. "Do you want me to?"

She had just finished her drink. "Making partner means a lot more money, which I believe you could do wonders with, but you've never seemed to care about money. I would support you with whatever decision you make."

He kissed her head. "You'd be the first who didn't tell me to take the money."

"That's not what I said. I just said I'd support you in whatever you decided." She snuggled back into his arms, and the two stared into the darkness. Allison pointed. "Look. A shooting star."

"I saw it. It was on our left, so that means bad luck."

Allison lifted her head. "I thought you wished on a shooting star."

"That's one thought. Another one is when you see a shooting star on your right side, it means good luck, but when you see it on the left, it means misfortune. Then there is the wishing on a star. I tend to believe in the wishing part. What would you wish for?"

A tear ran down her cheek. "That's simple. I wish to have your child."

He wiped away her tear with his knuckle. "You will."

"I hope so."

She lay back into his arms, and they gazed at the sky for another few minutes. "We should head back to shore," Chase said. He pulled the anchor out of the water, started the engine, and they headed back to the dock.

Fifteen minutes later, after they'd anchored the boat and were heading toward the Jeep, Chase's cell phone rang. He picked it up.

A male voice. "Chase Connor, hopefully you're not in your boat."

The blast knocked them to the ground.

Allison peered up. "They blew up your boat."

Chapter 10

Chase and Allison watched as the sheriff and his deputies searched through the wreckage. His arm remained around Allison's shaking shoulders.

"It's okay. We'll live to see another day."

Tears filled her eyes. "I don't know if I can't this."

"Take what?"

"Living on edge. It's too much—" They turned as Sophia ran toward them.

"Are you okay?" she said, hugging Allison.

"This time. We had just gotten off the boat when it blew up."

Sophia switched toward Chase. "I'm so sorry."

"Thanks, at least we weren't on the thing."

"Who would do something like this?" Allison asked.

Chase shook his head. "I have no clue, except for the voice on the phone."

They all turned to the sheriff who walked over. "Chase, let's go for a walk."

They walked away from the two ladies.

"What did you find, Sheriff?"

The sheriff took his hat off and rubbed his hair.

"There was enough dynamite onboard to blow you to kingdom come, but the question is why?"

"I can't answer that."

Sheriff Portal peered into his eyes. "You are very good at hiding your thoughts and feelings. I should have known better than to ask. Work with me here."

"Fine, Sheriff. Jonathan Gartner called me a few days after he was arrested telling me that the games had just begun. A minute before the explosion, a male voice—possibly Gartner—called to tell me it was a good thing we were off the boat."

"He's in prison in California. How could he do that? Better question, why would he want to do that?"

Chase shrugged. "The second question is easy for me to answer. He wants my billions. The first question is more difficult since I have no idea who knows him around here, other than the Shepherds. Nathan and Willis are in jail."

"Do you think Ophelia would do something like this?"

Chase shrugged again. "You know Mrs. Shepherd better than I do. Wish I could be more helpful. I'm clueless about what's happening, but I have my theories."

The sheriff sighed. "Your theories are what have helped me and others in this community figure out what's happening."

"Jonathan Gartner is a killer, and he'll do anything he can to stay out of jail. Since he has a slim chance of that happening, he'll destroy the one man who put him there. That's me. He'll be coming after everything that's important to me. The boat is a material thing, but it won't stop there."

"What can you do about it?"

Chase sighed. "I really don't know."

Once the sheriff left, Allison hurried over to him. "What is the sheriff going to do about it?"

"His job."

Allison glanced over at Sophia who was standing by herself, then turned back to Chase. "It's kind of interesting Sophia returns about the time this happens."

"You really believe she would have something to do with this?"

"Yes. You don't know the Shepherds as well as I do. They'd do anything to protect their own, and Sophia is no different than the others."

"What about their mother?"

Allison nodded. "That's a possibility."

Sophia peered up at them as they walked over. "What's next?" she asked.

Chase lifted a shoulder. "I'm going to continue running the bookstore and antique store like any other day. Sophia, will you bring my bride-to-be home? I need some time to think."

~

Allison turned to Sophia. "What a night."

"Are you okay?"

"I'm not sure how I feel about everything. I love Chase, but what's wrong with him that would make someone blow up his boat? Why can't he just sell books?"

"We both know that's not who Chase is. That's who you fell in love with."

Allison eyed Sophia. "I'm not sure about anything anymore. How about we have lunch tomorrow and talk about why you're back here, and what's happening with you and Kirby?"

"That would be nice. I've missed our times sitting down and talking about anything and everything."

They climbed into Sophia's car and headed back to Mountain Ridge. After Sophia dropped her off, Allison climbed the stairs to the apartment and dropped down beside Chase on the couch. "Really, reading a book after what happened tonight?"

Chase closed the book and peered at her. "It's who I am. I can't help it."

Allison went to the refrigerator to grab a beer. "Would you like one?"

"Yeah, that would be good."

She came out with two beers, opened the tops, and handed one to Chase. Dropping onto the couch, she took a large sip. Chase wrapped his arm around her. "I know this is all hard for you, but it'll work out."

She set her beer on a cabinet next to the couch. "There's a lot going on here, and I don't know if I can handle it. When I broke up with Willis, I was scared of what the Shepherds would do. Twice I've witnessed you almost being killed by a needle from some monstrous man. Then I discovered your hobby is helping the sheriff catch criminals, which in a way has landed you in this situation."

Allison grabbed her beer, took another drink, and set it back down. "And you're not the only problem. My father's situation is hard on me. Even though I've been away from him for ten years, I really felt like we could be a family again, I still believe that. Add to that the fact that there's a good chance I can't have a baby with you because of what happened." She locked eyes on him. "Finally, you asked me to marry you, but I don't feel like I did the night you proposed."

A frown spread across his face.

Tears brimmed her eyes. "I was so excited and happy about what was going to happen, but now I realize something will happen to you, and I'll be left alone once more. I don't know if I can handle that at all." She stood up and posted her hands on her hips. "Why can't you just run a bookstore like a normal man?"

Chapter 11

On Saturday, Sophia checked her watch before entering the bar and grill to meet Allison for lunch. Right on time. Once she was inside, she searched the facility, finally spotting Allison in a corner booth. She hurried over to her and slid down into the seat across from her.

"I'm glad you could make it," Allison said.

Sophia smiled. "How are you doing?"

"It's been tough, but I'm doing my best to work my way through it."

"I'm glad to hear that. I'm sure Chase has been there for you."

Allison sighed. "Actually, I've kept my distance from him for the last few days."

"Why would you do that?"

Allison picked up her water and sipped it. "He's a big reason why I feel like I do. In a way I feel like I did when I was with your brother. There's no escape."

"Don't feel like that. Chase is good for you."

They turned to Jake's voice. "Sophia Shepherd, I heard you were in town. You look different with brown hair. I like the change."

Sophia and Allison both laughed. "I didn't know you would keep tabs on me that closely," Sophia said.

Jake grinned. "When you see the most beautiful woman in Montana walk through your doors, you remember it."

"What would your wife say?" Sophia asked.

"I'd deny it and tell her she's the most beautiful woman in Montana. Anyway, today's lunch special is tuna sandwich with potato salad."

Both women went with the special with beers. Once he left, Sophia turned back to Allison. "Have you talked to Chase about all of this?"

"We have but all he can say is 'stay strong, and we'll work it out.'"

"Why don't you believe him?"

"I heard that from Willis."

Sophia sipped her water. "You realize those two are totally different men. I'd tend to believe Chase before I would my brother."

"I thought that too until I met his family. Granted they were nice to me the week I was there, but all the men, including their father, tried to pick me up, and they had no problems with it. In addition, they have ten security guards who watch over the whole family. How can anyone breathe like that? Sometimes I wonder if I jumped from one fire right into another."

Sophia frowned. "I'm sure seeing a boat blow up in front of your eyes scared you, but do you think maybe there is something more going on?"

Allison was quiet for a moment. "Yeah, there is a lot more going on."

"You already said you jumped from one fire into another. Do you love Chase because he helped you when you needed someone, or do you really love him?"

Allison finished taking a bite of her potato salad. "I'll have to think about it. What about you? Are you straightening everything out with your mom?"

"She's a wreck. If she saw Chase on the street, she'd run him over with her car or hit him with a slingshot."

Allison laughed. "A slingshot?"

"Yeah, anything that would dispose of him. I'm trying to help her understand that Chase has nothing to do with the choices our family makes. I've seen my Dad and Willis once since they were arrested. They aren't remorseful at all, and they still believe Gartner roped them in, but then they thought they were roped in for an earlier criminal offense. The mistake they made was going after Chase."

"What do you mean?"

Sophia finished sipping her beer. "I've met his brother, Micah, and sister, Samantha, in my tours down the runway in the past. They'll do anything to protect their little brother."

"That's true. Deep down I have this feeling Chase is the one who people need to fear. I have to admit Micah is one handsome dude."

"You may be right there." Sophia grinned.

Allison eyed her. "Did you spend time in the sack with Micah?"

"Never. Although I've made several mistakes in my life, I'm trying to be a better person."

"What happened with you and Kirby?"

Sophia finished part of her tuna sandwich. "It's simple. I never loved him. I've only loved one man, and he's gone."

"I'm sorry about Franklin being killed in that hit and run last year."

"Yeah, it was tragic."

They finished their lunch in silence until Allison glanced up to see Chase standing over them. "Sweetheart, what are you doing here?" Allison asked.

He sat down next to her. "Sophia, good to see you."

"You too, Chase."

He turned to Allison. "The sheriff wants me to meet him at the dock to go over some details. Do you want to join me?"

"No, I'm going to spend time with Sophia."

He kissed her on the forehead. "See you later."

~

Once Chase and the sheriff reached the dock, they sat there in the squad car.

"We're not checking the boat?" asked Chase, cutting Sheriff Portal a sideways glance.

"No. The demolition found the bomb was detonated remotely, meaning the person who set it off was nearby. We're pulling all the cameras in the area and checking them, but nothing yet."

"There's more."

He nodded. "A preliminary hearing is scheduled next week for the Shepherds, Gartner, and the others involved. There have been whispers the charges will all be thrown out because it's your word on what was said, and since it was dark no one could really get a good understanding of who was where, what was said—you name it."

Chase laughed. "Why does it not surprise me?"

"The bottom line is no one is clear about what

happened that evening, other than what you had to say. Everyone else's testimony matched."

"What about Deputy Samuels pointing a gun at me?"

"He says you made some strange movements, and he was protecting himself and the others."

Chance grimaced. "It's my fault."

"How is this your fault?"

"I should have rung Gartner's neck." Both were silent for a few minutes as they stared out at the lake. "Any more on the lady who fell down the mountain?" Chase asked.

"Still in a coma. Any more from the books?"

"Not yet, but I have been reading about some stuff near Creston and Echo Lake."

The sheriff sipped his coffee. "What's happening there?"

"Mount Aeneas has voices in the mountains."

Sheriff Portal laughed. "Now you're hearing voices?"

"I personally think it's the wind and the elevation which cause people to hallucinate and hear voices, but the other night, we heard the words as clear as day in both Native American and English."

The sheriff smiled. "To play along, what were they saying?"

"In English, soldiers from the past were complaining that they couldn't find the Native Americans they were tracking. I couldn't understand what else was said, but Edgar interpreted it for us saying they were thinking about attacking."

"Edgar Blacktail? He's always storytelling, so I don't know if I'd take much stock in what he has to say.

He also has this berry drink that he puts something into."

"Maybe so, but I know what I heard."

"What about Echo Lake?"

"The book I read talks about a lost girl at Echo Lake. I'm not sure what to think about that."

The sheriff pushed his hat back. "Eighteen months ago, there was a family in that area who vanished, a father and two daughters. It was in January, and no one could figure out what happened to them. We searched, found nothing, and figured they went back to where they came from."

"Do you remember the name?"

The sheriff frowned. "I haven't. Have you read that name?"

Chase nodded. "I remember reading in a mystery book about a group who was lost in the county, but all I remember is the location. I'll check into it. The problem is the mystery book is a couple of years old, so if you're saying eighteen months, why would that name be in it?"

"My timing may be off. I'll check the reports when I return and let you know. Right now, we'll keep digging into this boat blowing up."

Chapter 12

Once the sheriff dropped Chase off at the bookstore, Chase walked in to see Xavier stacking books.

"Good afternoon, Boss," Xavier said.

"How have things been going?"

"It's been busy already with many people coming in to search for a book about the history of Mount Aeneas. Do you know what's happening?"

"I don't. Were they Native American?"

"They were. We were able to find a couple of books online, so they ordered them. Strange because all of them ordered the same book."

Chase eyed Xavier. "That is weird. What was the book?"

Xavier checked the orders. "*Mysteries in the Mountains*. I ordered a copy for you since I figured you'd be interested in what's happening."

Chase laughed. "Thanks. Is Allison around?"

"No, she hasn't shown up yet."

"Thanks. I'll be outside if you need me." Chase sat down on a bench in front of the bookstore to think about everything that was happening. Allison was going to leave him and join her family in California. He had no clue what to do about the situation since it was the way his life had always gone. People were there, and then they weren't.

As far as those arrested, there was no question everyone would be released since it was Chase's word against everyone else's. For some reason it didn't bother him either, but then again this was his life. The boat blowing up was different. It was meant to be a warning. The thought should bother him, but for some reason it didn't.

Then there was Sophia. No question there were feelings between the two of them, and it would always be there. If the sheriff was correct, and she came back for him, it would make matters complicated all the way around. Even if Allison left, Sophia's family would make it difficult for the two of them. But then her family would make it difficult for him anyway.

He peered up at Allison and Sophia who stood on the sidewalk in front of him.

"Contemplating the adventures for the day?" Sophia asked, sitting down next to him.

"Yeah, you could say that."

Sophia's eyes darted from one to the other. "I'll see the two of you later."

"Take care," Chase said.

Allison took Chase's hands. "What's happening?"

He peered into her eyes. "There is a chance the Shepherds, or everyone for that matter, will be released from jail."

Her eyes widened. "How can that be?"

"My word against everyone else's. And it sounds like their stories match almost perfectly."

Allison stood up. "Why couldn't you just stay out of things?" She stomped into the bookstore.

What was that all about? Chase followed her in but ran into Xavier.

"One pissed off woman," Xavier said.

Chase couldn't help but laugh. "Yeah, it's been one of those days." He walked up the stairs to the apartment and found Allison in the bedroom throwing clothes into a suitcase. "What are you doing?"

She stopped and glanced at him. "I'm leaving this place like I should have several months ago."

Chase took her hand. "Calm down and let's talk about it."

The two sat on the edge of the bed, but she pulled her hand away. "No, Chase, there's no talking about it. I made a mistake getting hitched up with Willis, and it seems I've done the same thing with you."

Chase let out a breath. "I'll take the job in California with my family."

She popped her head up and peered into his eyes. "You would do that?"

"I love you."

She squeezed his hand. "And I love you, but it wouldn't matter if we were here or in California. As long as I'm with you, I'll never feel safe. Willis was mean. You're not mean, but there are so many people who want a piece of you, and I can't handle that. I worry enough the way it is about what happens to you. Can't imagine what it would be like when we have children, paparazzi, crazies—you name it. No, it's best I leave and join my family. I'm sorry."

She took off both her rings and handed them to Chase. "These belong to Sophia, and we both know that. She came back for you and nothing else." Allison stood and grabbed her bag. "The bus leaves in thirty minutes. Could you drop me off at the bus stop?"

"Are you sure this is what you want?"

She glanced at him. "It has to be this way for me. I can't bear to see anything happen to you, or me for that matter."

He drove her down to the bus station in Kalispell and followed her in, his hands stuffed in his pockets.

"I'll text you when I get to California to let you know I made it safely, but after that please move forward with your life and leave me alone. My sister's husband was transferred to Oregon, so I'll be with family."

When the bus pulled up, she gently kissed him. "This is goodbye. I wish you the best."

"You too."

He watched as she climbed onto the bus, found a window seat, and waved at him as the bus left. Chase stood there until the bus was out of sight. The Connor name was a curse, and he'd lost another woman who he could have a family with. It would never end!

Chapter 13

Chase was stacking books when a text came into his cell phone. It was from Allison who wrote that she'd arrived safely in Oregon. Her last sentence stated *this is goodbye*. He turned when the door opened, and Willis walked in, a look of triumph on his face.

"I'm out. I told you that no one could keep a Shepherd down."

Chase suppressed the urge to roll his eyes. "Are you here for a book?"

"No, I'm searching for Allison."

"If you're not here for a book, please leave."

Willis's smile vanished. "Where's Allison?"

Chase climbed down the ladder, walked over to him, and met his eyes. "I said if you aren't here for a book, please leave, and if you don't, I'll snap that pencil-thin neck of yours."

All the bravado escaped from Willis. He didn't say a word, turned, and hurried out the door. Chase shook his head. Willis was a piece of work, and he wasn't in the mood to deal with his stupidity.

That afternoon, the sheriff walked in. "I need something stronger than a cup of coffee."

Chase laughed. "I saw Willis earlier, so it means the preliminary hearing went badly."

"It did. All charges were dropped. The judge mentioned that it's quite amazing how close to perfect everyone's stories were. Right after that, Deputy Samuels turned in his badge and joined the Shepherds as a security guard."

"A security guard?"

The sheriff nodded. "Nathan Shepherd said he wants to avoid any reprisals from those in the community who believe he got away with a crime."

Chase laughed once more. "I'm sorry. This has turned into a joke."

The sheriff shook his head. "Deputy Samuels isn't the only one who thought about hanging it up. I seriously thought about it also, and I'm still thinking about it."

"I sure hope you don't because I'll miss working with you on these different mysteries."

The sheriff stood up to leave. "I have no idea what's going to happen with this group, so just beware."

Chase peered at him. "Anything done from this point will be behind the scenes, especially when it comes to Gartner. I can see him leaving the state and heading back to his old stomping grounds. He wants a sure thing."

After the sheriff left, Chase kept busy all afternoon with customers and ordering books. Chase had finished restocking the shelves for the evening and Milo had already turned on the closed sign when the door opened. "Sorry we're closed," Chase said.

"I know that. I stopped by to see how you were

doing."

Chase peered up at Sophia who was dressed in a stylish shirt, skirt, and knee-high boots. "It's bad enough your brother showed up this morning, and now your father is sending you. What do you want?"

She sighed. "I told you I just wanted to make sure you were okay. I take it Allison left?"

Chase glared at Sophia. "Please leave. I've had enough of the Shepherds for one day."

She didn't budge. He walked over to the door, locked it, then picked her up and set her on the desk.

~

"What are you doing?" Sophia said, as Chase lifted up her skirt. "Please stop. This is not you."

When she met his eyes, she saw something that she had never seen before. Pure hatred. "Please, don't force yourself on me. I won't stop you, but we both know that our lives will never be the same if you rape me."

He backed up a step.

She framed his face with her hands. "You are not your father or brothers, or my father or brother. Don't become like them. Please, let me go. All I wanted to do was check on you and invite you to dinner."

After he helped her off the desk, she straightened her skirt. "Are you hungry? I could cook you something."

"There isn't much upstairs."

"Let's see what you have." She took his hand, and the two walked upstairs. She went through his freezer. "I found two frozen dinners. Do you want spaghetti or teriyaki chicken?"

"Your choice."

She unwrapped them both and placed them in the

microwave. While they heated up, she found a half a bottle of chardonnay and poured two glasses. The microwave buzzer went off and she set the meals on the table.

"Some wine to go with dinner?"

Chase joined her at the table. "Thanks," he said softly.

They were both quiet as they ate their dinner. After dinner, Sophia cleaned up and joined Chase who was sitting on the love seat. She poured them each another glass of wine.

"Thanks," Chase said, glancing up at her.

"You're welcome." She set the wine on the table next to the love seat and sat down next to him.

He tasted his wine and then looked at Sophia. "I'm sorry about earlier."

She touched his hand. "I wasn't afraid. Like I said, if you forced yourself on me, I wouldn't have fought it, but we would have never been the same after that. I knew if I could reach you, we'd be okay."

She stopped for a sip of her wine. "I saw pure hatred in your eyes. Do you hate me that much?"

"Right now, I hate everything and everyone. Allison told me she would be there for me, and she left, just like you did, and other women have said and did the same thing. Then your family and a whole group of others have their charges dropped because they were able to get their stories straight. It boils down to the curse of being a Connor."

Sophia laughed. "I'm sorry, but you're being so melodramatic. You know better than that. I'm not speaking for the other women in your life, but you pushed me away. You are the only man I've ever been in love with. Remember the party when I came back last fall with my modeling manager? From the moment I saw you in the backyard, I knew you would always be in my heart."

A smirk covered his face.

She sipped her wine once more. "I came back specifically for you—not my father, my mother, brother, or anyone. Just you. I had hoped to rekindle what we'd lost. At the time I didn't know you were engaged to Allison."

"It doesn't matter anyway since she left for good."

She touched his hands. "I'm sorry for you. All I've wanted is for you to be happy."

He glared at her. "Is that what you really want? Or is it a way to help your family?"

"Whoa, don't you dare say that to me. I'm not like my family. Are you like yours? I can answer that for you. You're not, so what makes you think I can't be different from my family? I'm here tonight because I want to be here for you, as you were for me when I was hurting."

He didn't meet her eyes.

She touched his arm. "After Franklin was killed in that hit-and-run car accident, you held me all night, talked to me, soothed me. When I almost overdosed you stood over me most of the night gently talking to me. It wasn't Kirby or anyone else; it was you. I don't remember everything you actually said, but I do remember you telling me never to give up and at least twice, you whispered, 'please don't leave me.'"

He met her eyes. "You did."

"And whose fault was that? You're the one who pushed me toward Kirby believing all you'd do is cause problems because of your name. I don't care if your name is Connor; I just care about you."

She set her wine glass down, slid down on the couch, and stared up at the ceiling. "Every day I thought about you. Every night, I'd lie in bed and think about how our life was going to be. We'd be married. Have at least six children. The boys would be star athletes like their father, and the girls would cheer on their brothers like their mother did when she was younger." She turned to Chase. "I never told you that I was a cheerleader, did I?"

"You didn't. But six kids?"

She grinned. "At least six, but if we have more, I'm happy with that. The most important thing I want for our children is they become whatever they want to be, something that neither you nor I were able to do."

A light snore came from beside her.

A sideways glance showed Chase had fallen asleep. She reached down to take off her boots, then grabbed a blanket and covered the two of them up. "You were there for me when I needed you. Now I'll be there for you." She stroked his hair listening to his light snores. "Sleep tight, sweetheart. I promise I won't ever leave you again. You've heard that many times in your life, but this time it'll be true."

Chapter 14

Chase opened his eyes and peered at Sophia's face. The last he heard was her talking about their future life with children. It couldn't happen because he was a Connor. He gently climbed off the couch and walked into the bedroom to change clothes.

Before he left, he took one last gaze at her. He had to admit she was the most beautiful woman he had ever met, and when he saw her once more at the Fourth of July celebration, his heart beat faster than it ever had in his life. He quietly shut the door and padded down the stairs to open the bookstore.

Twenty minutes later Sophia joined him. "Good morning. Aren't you going to eat anything?" she asked.

"I wasn't hungry."

"I'll go down to the bar and grill to grab us something to eat."

Chase stopped her. "What is this?"

"I'm grabbing us breakfast. Is that okay?"

"It can't be more than that."

She let her breath out. "Why can't it be? We love each other deeply, and that's the way it will always be. But then if you don't feel that way, I'll wait, but believe me the two of us will be together forever. Right now, I'll grab you a breakfast sandwich and mocha."

"There will be no us. Thank you for last night, but please go on with your life."

She touched his hand. "I'll be back in a few minutes with breakfast."

After she left, Chase resumed stacking books. The door opened once more. "Back that soon?"

Standing there was Dr. Boyd. "Are you expecting someone?"

"Sophia was bringing me breakfast."

His eyes lit up. "You two are back together again?"

"We were never together, and no, we're not together."

Dr. Boyd laughed. "Funny, you must be the only one who doesn't know Sophia Shepherd is the one for you."

"What do you want?"

Dr. Boyd quickly scanned the bookstore. "You've done a wonderful job here. I stopped by to talk to you about a social event happening at my place tonight that I'd like you to attend."

Chase blew out a large breath. "Dr. Boyd, haven't you played enough games with me?"

"I don't know why you believe I'm playing games with you. All I've done is bring you to Montana to start these two businesses—which are going very well, I might add. This is a legitimate social event. Mr. Grenham will be there, and he asked that you join him to announce the opening of the Native American distribution center. You realize he's added yet another distribution company to a conglomerate of companies in the region?"

"Why didn't he ask me himself?"

Dr. Boyd sighed. "He's been awfully busy, so I told him I'd contact you. Besides, you should have received an invitation."

"I haven't checked the mail in a couple of days."

Dr. Boyd grinned once more. "Maybe you should check your mail once in a while."

"Maybe I should. Is that all?"

Dr. Boyd eyed him. "You've gone through a lot in your life, but you know as well as I do that the Connor name is a big reason for that. No matter what you believe right now, you've accomplished things that are yours alone. The bookstore, the antique store, mystery solving, even connecting with Sophia. She just doesn't fall in love with anyone, but she did fall in love with you."

Chase glared. "Enough. You relayed the message about tonight, so if you aren't going to buy a book, please leave."

"Don't change who you are."

Right after he left Sophia came through the door. "Dr. Boyd didn't look so happy. Did you piss him off?"

"Thanks for the breakfast. I have to get to work."

"So do I. I'm meeting the new realtor in town. I purchased the realty business from Mr. Hamilton, so I'll be a couple blocks away. We can spend lunch together, dinner, breakfast—you name it."

Chase rolled his eyes. "Nothing is going to happen with us."

She giggled. "Not right now, but it will. I'll keep an eye out for a house that will fit our needs in the future. See you later." She winked at him as she left.

Throughout the day, Chase kept busy with people

coming in and out searching for books. There were many new customers, some from as far away as Missoula. One such man stopped in right after lunch.

Chase was curious. "Why would you drive from Missoula to find a book on the environment when you have a wonderful library on campus?"

"Professor Littrel told his colleagues this is a place to find rare books, so I'd thought I'd stop by. Besides, it's only a couple of hours' drive, classes are out for the summer, and I do love this part of the country." He stuck out his hand. "By the way, my name is Professor Allan Stewart, and I teach environmental courses on campus."

"Nice to meet you, sir. I do have a question for you. Can the environment cause a person to hear noises in the mountains?"

"Of course. There are at least four environmental factors that I know of, but there are probably more."

"Would you like a cup of coffee?"

"I'd love one," the professor smiled.

A few minutes later, Chase came back out with two cups of coffee along with sugar packets and creamers.

"Thanks," the professor said. While he was doctoring his coffee, he started talking. "One factor is the acoustic effects of the mountain terrain. For instance, sound waves can bounce off rocks, create echoes, and amplify certain frequencies." He took his first sip. "Very good coffee. Then there are altitude and air density. As you ascend higher into the mountains, air density decreases which means that thinner air can affect how sound travels. The lack of oxygen can also cause hallucinations including auditory ones. But then this occurs usually over 23,000 feet, and there are no mountains in this area that high."

He lifted three fingers. "Another factor could be wind. For example, strong winds in mountainous areas carry sound over long distances, and also can distort it. Then such things as temperature inversions, where warm air traps cooler air near the ground, can create sound ducts. This would allow distant sounds to travel farther."

Chase piped up. "Professor, you're saying we could be at one location, hear a noise, but it could be many miles away from where we are?"

"Correct. Why are you so curious about all of this?"

Chase set down his cup. "I read books all the time and I dive into mysteries from these books. For example, I've read something about what some have called a 'triangle' that includes Creston, Mount Aeneas, and Echo Lake. A Kootenai man joined me and my former fiancée in the mountains, and we heard voices, but we weren't exactly sure where they were coming from. Could that happen?"

"Absolutely. However, let me be clear there are also psychological factors that can play a part in this. Isolation and quietness in mountains can heighten perception, which means people can become attuned to subtle sounds leading to auditory illusions. In addition, loneliness or fear can also influence how we interpret sounds. This means you could be hearing things that aren't there."

Chase nodded. "Makes sense."

"You said something about a triangle. Did you find anything in the other two places — Creston and Echo Lake?"

"Nothing in Creston, but Echo Lake is the one that concerns me the most."

"What do you mean?"

Chase sighed. "Like I said I'm really into books, and I came across a portion of one of the books that talks about voices near Echo Lake. Then I found out that a family was last seen there about eighteen months or so ago, but they disappeared. No one is sure if something happened to them or if they just returned home. The thing is there's a girl's voice that has been heard in an area of Echo Lake."

"Is it near the mountain?"

"Nope."

"Have you been out there?"

"Once, but we didn't hear the voice. The Kootenai man we were with had heard it before."

"This is quite interesting. Would you mind driving me out to that area?"

"I can't right now, but tomorrow I could."

"I'd have to find a place to stay for the evening, but I'd be willing to do that. In fact, I'll call Professor Littrel and have him join us tomorrow."

"You can stay in my apartment. I have an extra bed."

"That would be great."

"In fact, I have to close up and get ready for a social event tonight. Would you like to join me?"

The professor laughed. "Am I dressed appropriately?"

Chase laughed. "You see how I'm dressed."

Chapter 15

It was after seven when Chase and Professor Stewart arrived at the Boyds'. The first thing they did was grab a glass of wine off a tray from a lady that was walking by. The professor laughed. "One good thing about these social events—There's always plenty of wine and nice-looking women. Wow, that one is a beauty."

Chase shifted to see the object of Stewart's ogling. Ah, Sophia. Dressed in a strapless blue dress and the same knee-high boots from earlier in the day, she wore her hair in an elegant updo. The professor was right; she was a beauty,

"Do you know her?" Stewart asked.

"Yes, that's Sophia Shepherd."

"Ah, Shepherd. I've heard that name in and out of the news. Recently, one of them was just released from prison. Before his incarceration, he was hoping to build a resort in this area of Montana. That never materialized."

Dr. Boyd joined the two. "Who do we have here, Chase?"

"This is Professor Allan Stewart. He's an environmental professor at the University of Montana."

"Nice to meet you," Dr. Boyd said, shaking his hand. "Interesting you'd be at this event."

"Chase invited me. I was searching for some books at the bookstore, we got to talking about things, and he said he had to go, so here we are."

Dr. Boyd sipped his wine. "Nice to meet you. Please enjoy yourself." He turned to Chase. "Mr. Grenham is waiting to talk to you before he makes his announcement."

"What are you talking about?"

Dr. Boyd shifted toward the professor. "Could you excuse us?"

"Sure. Think I'll mosey over and strike up a conversation with that beauty over there."

Dr. Boyd and Chase ambled over to where Mr. Grenham was talking to a couple. "Mr. Grenham, I found Chase."

He turned to Chase and proffered his hand. "It's nice to see you once more." Grenham nodded toward the couple who stood next to him. "This is Mr. and Mrs. Claude Bottoms, who are working with me on this new idea you came up with."

"Nice to meet you both," Chase said.

The man smiled at him. "Same here. Donald said you're going to start a reading program in both the bookstore and on the reservation, is that right?"

"That is the hope, with Mr. Grenham's help. His distribution network will help immensely."

"It will," he said. "Maybe you can explain to me how it's going to work."

Chase took a sip of his merlot. "The Native American culture plays a prominent role in this area, but sadly, there is so much we don't know about their culture. I'm proposing to start reading classes in the bookstore and on the reservation that would bring different books about the Native American culture into focus. Granted there are books on Native Americans in both locales, but there is little discussion between the two groups of what the culture is all about."

Mr. Grenham smiled at his wife. "You see, Eloise. From his lips to God's ears."

Good. They were on board. He continued. "For instance, we could choose a book dealing with different types of foods from both cultures and offer a unique culinary experience for the county's citizens to try. Sort of like the booth displays in the convention center, on the reservation, or even on the streets of the communities."

Mr. Bottoms nodded toward Mr. Grenham. "Count us in."

"Great," he said, slapping Bottoms on the back. "Let's get this started,"

Once they walked away, Chase turned to Dr. Boyd. "Who are they?"

"Bottom's a big shot on all the reservations in Montana and has a lot of pull. Now that he's involved, this plan will work. Let's go."

"Go where?" Chase asked.

"Up to the front with the rest of the group. After all, this is your plan."

Chase huffed, "I have a big mouth."

They joined the others on a makeshift stage in the Boyds' house. Chase found Sophia standing next to the professor when she waved her fingers at him. He returned the wave then turned to Dr. Boyd who introduced those involved in the project. "Please welcome Mr. Grenham." He clapped and left the stage.

The distinguished man with black hair, graying at the temples, and glasses took front and center. He seemed to belong in this environment. "I'm happy to be up here talking to you all about this project and reaching out for financial support. Actually, I had no intention of talking to Chase Connor, since I can't stand anyone in his family—" He paused until the snickers stopped. "—so I figured Chase was no different. I was completely wrong. Chase Connor has it together and has come up with a wonderful idea. This is all his idea, and I'll let him tell you about it."

Chase slowly walked toward the podium. He covered the microphone with his hand and whispered something to Grenham. The man laughed. Chase stood in front of the microphone. "As I told Mr. Grenham, I felt like I was roped into this. And as he said, 'You opened your big mouth.'"

It drew a laugh from the group.

"He's right, I did open my big mouth, but I thought it would be a good thing for the Native American population and those who live in the county with them to get to know each other. At times, I think we're still at war, which is sad after all these years. Part of it is because we just don't understand where each other is coming from, so maybe this will help out."

He peered over at Sophia. She was smiling, and her eyes glowed. Her presence helped calm him down. He turned to the audience and explained what was happening with the program. After he was finished, he said, "I'll take any questions."

One lady wondered about the types of events that would be offered. "My idea is to take a book and use it as a reference to something more. For example, as I told Mr. and Mrs. Bottoms, we could focus on recipes from both cultures, cook favorite foods, and offer small plates at kiosks at different county events. There could be many other ideas."

Over the next fifteen minutes, Chase answered questions about the project. When it was over, Chase stepped down and hurried out the door. He stepped outside into the Boyds' yard and took a deep breath. He peered up at Sophia who approached.

"You were wonderful. Scared, but wonderful."

Chase laughed. "I thought my chest was going to burst out."

She touched his hand. "You're through now, and I'm proud of you. I understand Professor Stewart is spending the night with you, and you two are going to check out some voices at Echo Lake?"

"Yeah, tomorrow."

Sophia grinned. "He asked me to join him for a drink after the event tonight. When I asked him where, he said your apartment. Are you renting out your apartment now for visitors' rendezvous?" She laughed when Chase's cheeks warmed.

"I'm sorry about that."

She squeezed his hand. "Don't be. I kindly told him that I had someone else I was interested in, but he did invite me to join you and Professor Littrel on your Echo Lake adventure tomorrow."

"And?"

"Of course, I accepted, since I'll be with you, and you'll keep me out of harm's way."

"Yeah, right, like I did Allison."

She sighed. "That was not your fault."

He tipped his head toward the professor who was quickly approaching.

"There you are, Ms. Shepherd," Professor Stewart said, hurrying over to them. "That was a great talk, Chase. I'm going to talk to the professors at the university about finding ways to be part of this. I don't know how, but I'll see what we can do." He turned to Sophia. "I wanted to make you aware that we'd be leaving at ten in the morning. Professor Littrel will be here by nine."

Sophia smiled. "How about if I bring breakfast for you all."

"That would be wonderful," Professor Stewart said. "I should ask Chase if that's okay."

"It is. She's a wonderful cook."

The professor grinned once more. "I should have asked Ms. Shepherd if it would be a problem accompanying three men around a lake unchaperoned."

She eyed Chase. "Chase will make sure nothing happens to me. I should get going since tomorrow is going to be a long day. Good night, Professor Stewart. You too, Chase."

Once she had left, Professor Stewart whistled. "She is a beauty. I can see myself falling for someone like her."

"Aren't you in your forties?"

"Forty-two to be exact, but we're in Montana, and age means nothing. Women like her love to meet up with older men. It'll take time but I'll keep trying. In fact, I already plan on spending more time in this area of the state."

"And if she has eyes for someone else?"

The man grinned. "I can change her mind."

Chapter 16

It was after nine when Professor Littrel arrived at the bookstore. Sophia peered up as she dished up breakfast pizza and alerted Chase to his arrival.

"What happened to your fiancée?" he asked Chase when he along with Professor Stewart joined him at the front of the store.

"It didn't work out. Come, join us for breakfast."

"All right. I'm sorry to hear that about your fiancée. Isn't this Sophia Shepherd?"

"One and the same," Sophia said, cutting him a piece of breakfast pizza. "I hope this is large enough."

"It looks wonderful. I'm hungry, so I may eat more."

"There's plenty to eat," Sophia said. She cut herself a piece and joined them at the table.

Professor Littrel bit into his pizza. "This is amazing. You made it, Sophia?"

"From scratch. It's the first time I ever made a dish like this, but I wanted to make sure you guys were full before you hit the lake."

"You're not joining us?" Professor Stewart asked.

She peered over at Chase and then back to the

professor. "Do you still want me to join you?"

"Of course, I do, if it's okay with Chase. It's his expedition."

Chase had just finished a portion of his pizza. "I'd hope she would join us since it would be great to get a woman's perspective on what's happening. By the way, this is wonderful. You can do all my cooking."

She smiled. "Are you sure that's what you want?"

They all laughed when Chase blushed. He patted his stomach. "It's very good. Let's leave it at that."

A few minutes after ten, they climbed into Chase's Jeep and made the drive toward Echo Lake. When they pulled into the lake area, Edgar was waiting for them.

"I got your message, Chase," Edgar said when he joined them.

Chase gestured toward the local man. "This is Edgar Blacktail. He lives on the lake and has heard the sounds we're talking about."

Professor Littrel studied the Native man. "Interesting. Do you hear the sounds often?"

Edgar sipped his canteen. "Maybe every couple of weeks. But at times it could be more frequent."

Professor Littrel turned to Chase. "What's the plan? You're in charge here."

"Let's break up into two teams. Edgar, do you feel like working with Professor Littrel on the south end of the lake, and we'll take the north end?"

"Sounds like a plan."

Professor Stewart grinned. "A wonderful plan."

Chase, Sophia, and Allan headed toward the north side of the lake. As they walked, Allan stayed close to Sophia.

"Where did you go to school?"

"University of Montana," she said. "I have a business degree. And you're a professor at the university?"

"Yes, in environmental sciences. I drove down yesterday to check out Chase's store since many people have said he has a good collection of rare books on display."

"Any luck?" Sophia asked.

"I did find a couple of books that will be useful. What do you do?"

"I took over as the realtor in Mountain Ridge."

"Do you work outside of Mountain Ridge?"

She nodded. "My license takes me all over the county."

They stopped when Chase did. He pointed toward a grove of trees. "Is that a bear?" the professor asked.

"It is," Chase said. He took out his cell phone and took some photos as the bear wandered down toward the lake. He crawled in and started sipping the water. Just like that he stuck out his paw, grabbed a trout, and ate it. Once finished, the bear plodded down the beach in their direction.

"What do we do?" the professor asked.

Chase stopped in his tracks as Sophia squeezed behind him. "Stay calm and do not run."

"Are you sure that's a good idea?" Sophia asked, her hand on his shoulder.

He twisted his head toward her. "Have I let you down? Never mind, don't answer that question."

The bear continued lumbering their way. Maybe twenty feet away he stopped and stared at them.

"Don't look into his eyes," Chase said. "If he gets any closer, make lots of noise. Make yourself as big as possible, but don't run!"

The bear stood up and roared. Once he didn't get any response from the group, he turned toward and made his way into the trees. Once it was deep in the forest, Sophia wrapped her arms around Chase. "Thank you."

Chase blew out a breath. "I think it's safe now. Let's walk." They traveled another hour when Sophia stopped them. "I heard something."

"Where? What?" Chase asked.

She pointed. "Up there."

"Let's take a look," Chase said, leading the way.

They traveled into the trees and saw some footprints. The professor bent down to study them. "They could be a girl or woman's footprints. They're that small."

Chase pulled out his cell phone and texted the sheriff.

"What did you do?" Sophia asked.

"I asked the sheriff how old the kids were that were lost a couple of years ago."

They continued down the path when the text came back. Chase stopped to read it. "The girls were in their teens."

"What else did he say?" Sophia asked.

Chase grinned. "He asked if I needed to be on standby."

Sophia laughed. "He knows you so well."

They both could tell the professor was confused. Chase explained. "I seem to get myself into trouble at times, and the sheriff has to bail me out."

"You could have told me beforehand."

"I didn't think about it. Now you know."

They continued walking up the trail single file with Chase in the lead and the professor bringing up the rear. After another twenty minutes, Chase stopped. "Let's take a break."

"I need it," the professor said. "I'll be right back."

Once he was gone, Sophia touched Chase's arm. "The guy has been watching my ass the last thirty minutes. Is he a pervert?"

"Don't know that. I do know he has the hots for you."

She sighed. "Why won't you have the hots for me, so no one else will?"

He started to say something when they both heard a girl's voice. They stared at each other wide-eyed. "Did the girl say, 'Sophia, save us.'?"

Sophia visibly swallowed. "That's what I heard also."

"It makes me wonder if you're connected to her in some way? Do you know any other people in the area that have your name?"

She shook her head. "I can't think of anyone, but that doesn't mean a thing."

They shifted their attention to a noise coming from the trees. The professor was racing out of the trees. "Why didn't you tell me there were skunks in the area?"

Chase and Sophia both pinched their noses. "Wow, Professor, you took the full brunt of the skunk. You are rank," Chase said. "We're done for now. The trail ends up just ahead. Sophia and I will see what's up there. Maybe it would be best if you took a walk into the lake. Here's some soap to clean yourself up."

"You carry soap?" the professor asked.

"Among other things. When I first came to Montana, I wasn't sure what to expect, so I gathered anything I could think of to keep me alive, especially blankets and anything else that could keep me warm."

The professor laughed. "I'm just glad you have soap. I'll see you two back at the lake."

Once he left, Chase and Sophia continued up the trail. They had walked another quarter of a mile or so when the trail ended at a grove of trees. Chase checked to see if he could find any footprints. "Nothing," he said, peering up at Sophia.

"We both heard the voice. Who could it have been?"

Chase shrugged. "It has to be someone else named Sophia. It's hard to imagine they would know who you are, if you have no idea who they are."

"Not necessarily. My family has so many business dealings, so it's possible that there is someone else named Sophia among them." When Chase was silent, Sophia took his hand. "What are you thinking? I know that look."

He sighed. "What if your mother or father had an affair, and you have sisters that you don't know about."

She backed up a step. "That wouldn't surprise me, but let's not jump to conclusions." She continued holding his hand as the two retraced their steps. "I enjoyed today exploring with you. Even with the bear, I wasn't scared."

He laughed. "That's why you stayed behind me?"

She smirked. "While he was eating you, I was going to run as fast as I could."

"Thanks. I appreciate that."

She stopped, turned him around, and peered into

his eyes. "I told you I would never leave you, and I meant it." She framed her hands gently around his face and kissed him gently. "I wanted to do that more than anything, but you said it wouldn't happen, so I'll go see if my date is done bathing himself."

Chapter 17

After they emerged from the trees, they joined Edgar and Professor Littrel who were watching Allan swim around in the lake with his clothes on.

Edgar rolled his eyes. "Are all professors weird?"

They all laughed. Chase explained, "He ran into a skunk who took a liking to him. Any luck on your end?"

"Nothing," Professor Littrel said. "And you?"

Chase wiped his forehead. "We heard a girl's voice say something. Edgar, you said you had heard voices around here before. What did they say?"

"'Help me.' What did you hear?"

"The same," Chase said. "Are you sure there's no one else around here?"

Edgar stroked his whiskers. "There are several people who live in the area, but I can't think of any who have young children. Most are older folks like me who are retired or people who want to be on their own. I'll have to think about it more."

They turned to Professor Stewart's voice as he walked out of the lake. "Now that was refreshing. Thanks for the soap, Chase. I feel brand new. You ought to try jumping in the lake with your clothes on with a bar of soap. It's quite different."

They headed back to Edgar's house and sat around an outdoor campfire. Edgar grilled some burgers and provided the group some of his berry drink.

"This tastes awfully good," Professor Stewart said. "I know there are berries in it, but what else do you stick in it that gives it the alcoholic taste?"

Edgar was stone-faced. "Just berries."

Professor Stewart turned to Chase. "We didn't really accomplish anything today, did we?"

Chase shook his head. "Maybe it's just one of those days where there were no voices. Edgar said he doesn't hear them every day."

"I don't," Edgar agreed. "I've been trying to think if there was a certain day, a type of weather—anything like that, but I can't come up with a thing."

Chase sipped his drink. "Have you ever heard the name, Sophia, or some name associated with that name?"

Again, Edgar thought for a moment. "Other than Sophia Shepherd? I can't think of any name like that. I'm sorry. On another note, did you find anything more out about the mountain?"

"Nothing," Chase said. "Both are dead ends. I'm not too concerned about the mountains, but I'm more worried about the young girl. There is someone up there needing help."

Professor Littrel finished eating his burger. "In that mystery book, there were a few paragraphs about a family lost in the lake during a winter snowstorm. They were never found, so everyone thought they had just gone back home or fell into the lake and drowned."

"I'll read back through that portion and maybe check some other spots."

Professor Littrel stood up. "If it's okay with you, Chase, I really need to get on the road."

They climbed into the Jeep and drove back to Mountain Ridge. Once they reached the town, the professors hopped into their cars for the trip back to Missoula. Chase and Sophia stood outside the bookstore.

"I should head home, also," Sophia said. "I have some things to do before I head to work tomorrow. Like I said earlier, I had a wonderful day today. I'll talk to you soon."

Chase strolled with her to her car. He opened the door for her, and she climbed in.

"You are always such a gentleman. I'll see you when I can."

~

Sophia arrived back at her family's house, parked the car, and walked into the house. She headed straight up to her bedroom, closed the door, and dropped on the bed staring up at the ceiling. Sophia felt better about what was happening between her and Chase. They would be okay.

Sophia went into her bathroom, started the bathwater, and came back out to the bedroom to strip down for a soaking hot tub. She had walked more today than she had in a long time, and she was feeling it. Stepping into the tub, she leaned against the edge, closed her eyes, and relaxed.

As the jets were massaging her, she thought about the voice she and Chase had heard. It was a girl's voice and they both heard her say, "help us, Sophia." It seemed like the voice was so real, not like what people had said they heard in the mountains.

She turned to her cell phone when a text went off. She dried her hands, then reached over to check it. *I'll be in Mountain Ridge in a couple of days so we can talk. We need to straighten everything out.*

She typed a return text. *Don't bother. We're through.*

And she was through with Kirby, but then she had never started a relationship with the guy since her heart had always belonged to Chase. Now she just had to help him understand that she was the one woman who would not leave him and break his heart.

She climbed out of the tub, dried herself, and pulled up shorts and a t-shirt. Slipping into a pair of sandals, she walked downstairs to the pool area where everyone was sitting. "What do we have here?" Sophia asked.

"Sophia, I'm glad you're back. You remember most everyone here. Also with us are Mr. and Mrs. Holland. They run a technology company based out of Salt Lake City."

"What brings you to Montana?" Sophia asked.

Mr. Holland finished sipping his wine. "Opportunity. We're searching for a different lifestyle for ourselves and our employees, and we like what we see here in Montana."

"Welcome."

"Thank you," Mrs. Holland said. "Your mother was saying you run the realty company here?"

"I do."

Mr. Holland interrupted. "Do you practice commercial real estate? We're looking for a building and property to relocate the business. Would you have a suitable location?"

"It depends on what you're looking for."

"Our son will arrive tomorrow. He'll provide you with all the details," Mr. Holland said. "You might like him."

Sophia smiled. "I'm calling it a night. It was wonderful meeting you. If your son wants to stop by the office after ten, I'll see what I can do for you." Sophia said her goodbyes, then hurried to her room. She slipped into a nightgown and crawled into bed. Her last thought before she fell asleep was Chase holding her in his arms.

Chapter 18

Chase's eyes popped open, and he smelled something cooking in the kitchen. He crawled out of bed and slipped on a T-shirt. Walking out of the bedroom, he stopped when he saw Sophia cooking on the stove. "What are you doing?"

She glanced over her shoulder. "I'm making you breakfast. Today we're having pancakes, and they're about ready. Good morning."

Chase sat down at the table as she dished out two pancakes on a plate. She placed it on the table in front of him, filled a plate for herself, and joined him.

"What are you doing?" Chase asked.

She smiled. "I'm eating breakfast."

"How did you get in here, and why are you cooking me breakfast?"

"Both answers are quite simple. Remember you gave me a key? As to question two, you seem to forget to eat breakfast, so I decided to provide you some nourishment first thing in the morning."

He grinned. "You're becoming a domesticated woman."

She returned the smile. "Whatever it takes to keep

you in my life. Any big plans this morning?"

"Other than hopefully selling books, no, how about you?"

"I will meet with my first client sometime today. I met Mr. and Mrs. Holland at my parents' house last night. Their son is coming to town today to look for a space for a new technology business."

"You'll like Toby."

Her eyes widened. "Do you know him?"

"Yeah, he's one of Micah's best friends. They went to school together at Stanford. While Micah was struggling to become a lawyer, Toby was acing his technology classes."

"Interesting. Do I have to worry about him being another criminal my dad is hooking up with?"

Chase laughed. "Not everyone we deal with is a criminal."

"That's true. You're not."

Chase swallowed a bite, then put down his fork. "You'll like him. He's intelligent, well-mannered, and handsome."

"So are you and much more. Besides, I'm not interested in any other man. I've found the one I want to spend my life with."

Chase's eyes lost their sparkle. "It won't happen."

She reached over to lift his face. "It will happen." She climbed out of her chair. "I should get going. Have a wonderful day, and I'll see you later. I won't join you for lunch, but maybe we can have dinner together tonight. Pizza in Kalispell?"

He laughed. "You don't give up, do you?"

"Never again." She slipped around the table, wrapped her arms around his head, and kissed him. "I know you do love me as I do you." She whirled around to head for the stairs.

"You do look nice today."

She spun around in her skirt, light blue blouse, and ankle boots and curtsied. "Thank you."

Once he heard the door shut, he climbed out of the chair, walked into the bedroom, and sat down on the edge of the bed. Running his hands through his hair, he thought about Sophia. She was right, he had loved her once, but he was afraid that he would break her heart someway, somehow.

He had thought he and Allison would be a good pair, but that had gone wrong in the end. It was all about fear for Allison. She was always afraid of the Shepherds, as well as worried about something happening to him. It was too much for her, and he didn't blame her for going elsewhere. He just hoped she would find some happiness in her life.

He stripped down, then climbed into the shower. Once finished he got dressed for the day. He walked down the stairs to find Milo already boxing some the items from a shelf in the antique store.

"Good morning, Chase," the older man said.

"Same to you. You're awfully early."

"Yeah, it's time to change the display. I'm thinking about an August theme tied into the medical field, since it's Neurosurgery Outreach month, Psoriasis Awareness month, and Spinal Muscular Atrophy Awareness month."

Chase jumped in. "So, you're going to display some of our antique medical equipment and tie it into the theme?"

"You're learning also. Good for you."

Chase grinned. "It's helpful that you make it understandable when you talk about the displays."

"Thanks. I hate to kick you out, but I have to get to work."

"Understood. I'm going to do some reading myself." Chase chose a couple of books to see if he could find out any more about the incident at Echo Lake. Ten minutes after reading, he ran across a passage talking about a family that included two girls in it. Could this be it?

He read some more and ran across a few names. Gene and Evelyn Clinton had two daughters, Eleanor and Jenny. They went missing two years ago and were presumed dead, although it couldn't be verified since no bodies were found.

After finding out the family was last seen on the south side of Echo Lake, he closed the book and called the sheriff.

He answered after the second ring. "What are you getting me into now?"

"Can you meet me at Echo Lake near Edgar Blacktail's cabin in thirty minutes?"

"I can meet you there in forty-five. I have to finish something up."

"Sounds good. I have an idea where those voices may be coming from. While I'm waiting for you, I'll go grab Edgar also."

Chase climbed in his Jeep, drove down Main Street, and out toward Echo Lake. He landed at Edgar's cabin thirty minutes later. The old man was sitting outside smoking a questionable substance that reeked. Chase joined him.

"Would you like a hit?"

Chase laughed. "Sorry, Edgar, I don't do that sort of stuff."

"Maybe you should try it. You could use something to calm down your wired body."

"Yeah, I've heard that from a couple of other people. I'm really not that excitable, but at times situations get me wired. I may have found out the names of those who were lost at Echo Lake."

Edgar's eyes widened. "Oh?"

"Yes, Gene and Evelyn Clinton had two daughters. They went missing two years ago, and are presumed dead. Have you heard that name?"

"I have. They were regulars, and what I mean by regulars is they would come out each summer to do some hiking, fishing, and the little girls would always be in the lake swimming. Nice family."

"How did you get to know them?"

Edgar blew out smoke. "They hired me to take them out to where the fish are. I do a lot of fishing in the lake. Can't ever remember them showing up in the winter months. It was strictly summer." Edgar took a toke then spoke again. "Two years ago was different because the wife came out with the two girls but not the husband in the summer. I don't know if there is anything with that, but that's what happened. Wait, I was wrong. They did come one winter, but it was the father who was with the girls, not the mother, if I remember correctly."

Chase eyes widened. "Marital problems possibly?"

"Could be."

The sheriff drove up. Edgar quickly snuffed out his joint.

The sheriff hopped out of his vehicle. "This had

better be good."

Chase laughed. "You enjoy getting out of the office."

Sheriff Portal growled. "Good morning, Edgar. Are you causing any problems today?"

"Nope, Chase and I were just having a nice conversation when you showed up."

The sheriff sniffed, eyed him, then focused his attention on Chase. "What do you have?"

"I'm not sure, but it could be something. The book I was reading said that Gene and Evelyn Clinton were up here two years ago with their two girls but were either missing or presumed dead. Edgar remembers the names well because he did some fishing with them. That summer the mother showed up with the two kids but not the father, then the father was with them during that winter when they supposedly disappeared."

The sheriff moaned. "I remember that. We were out here in the middle of January searching for bodies but found nothing. We didn't know that the wife wasn't with them at that time."

"Could she still be alive?" Edgar asked.

The sheriff grabbed his cell phone. "We'll see." He called the sheriff's department. "Find out what you can about Evelyn Clinton." He shut the phone down and turned back to the other two. "What am I doing here?"

Chase grinned. "We're taking a hiking trip into the woods."

When the sheriff growled for the second time, Chase grinned. "You really ought to have eaten something before you came up here."

"Aw, shut up and let's go."

The three headed toward the north end of the lake.

Once Chase found the trail, they hiked toward the mass of trees where Chase had stopped a day or so before.

The sheriff's phone rang and brought them to a halt. He answered it and listened. There were a bunch of "okays," "really," and then "thanks." He pocketed his phone and turned to Chase and Edgar. "Evelyn Clinton is dead. She died in a car wreck in Washington eighteen months ago."

"Doesn't that seem strange?" Chase asked.

"It does. Let's go down this trail to see what we can find."

They continued for another ten minutes before they arrived at the large grove of trees. "This is where we stopped when we were here," Chase said.

"Let's move forward a bit more," the sheriff said.

It was slow going through the heavy growth of trees and vegetation. "I don't remember it being this dense up here," Edgar said.

Twenty minutes later they came out into an opening. Sitting in front of them was a small cabin with swings on the outside, as well as a round swimming pool. "It looks like someone lives here," Chase said.

"Let's go find out," the sheriff said.

They walked closer when a gun exploded in front of them. "That's far enough. This is private property."

The sheriff spoke up. "I'm Sheriff Portal of the Flathead County Sheriff's Department. Put the gun down and let's talk."

"There will be no talking."

Just like that the door flew open, and out ran a thin girl with scraggly hair. "Save us." Another gun blast went off hitting the girl in the leg. She fell down immediately. "Girl, you know better."

The sheriff spoke up once more. "Gene Clinton? I'll call in the department, and this will be a bloody bath."

"Then let it be because no one is taking my daughters from me. My wife tried that a couple of years ago." A tall lanky man with a beard down to his waist came out onto the small porch, a rifle trained on them.

"At least let us help the little girl. She's bleeding," Chase said.

"That's her own fault. She's thirteen, and she knows the rules up here."

The man aimed his gun one more time, but just as he was about to pull the trigger, another girl came from behind him, plunged a knife into the side of his leg, and flew off the porch toward the other girl. He screeched and fell down as his leg gave way.

While the man was trying to get up, Chase scrambled for the little girl lying on the ground. He scooped her up and raced back to the others. The sheriff stepped forward, his gun aimed at the man on the porch.

"It's over. Stay down, or I'll put a bullet between your eyes."

The man tried to get up once more but fell down and dropped the rifle. His leg was bleeding badly. The sheriff cautiously approached. Once he was close enough, he kicked the rifle out of the way. "Gene Clinton, you're under arrest for shooting at a sheriff, attempted homicide of the girl, and endangering the life of two youngsters."

"They're my daughters."

"We'll figure that out." The sheriff took out his cell phone and called the department asking for backup.

Once he was off the phone, Gene Clinton growled.

"Aren't you going to do something about my leg?"

"As soon as I get you restrained to make sure you don't try anything." Once the sheriff had handcuffed the man, he checked the wound. "Looks like you'll survive. You had better hope nothing has happened to your daughter." He jumped off the porch. "Is she okay, Chase?"

Chase lifted his eyes. "She needs a doctor. The bullet is lodged in her leg, she's bleeding, and she's out like a light."

"Let's get her back to the vehicle as quickly as possible."

Chase lifted her up, then hurried away, the other young girl racing behind him.

"I'll stay with the sheriff," Edgar said.

Once Chase was back in the trees, he found the trail once more.

"Is my sister going to be okay?"

"We'll have to see once we get her to a doctor."

"I'm glad that someone came to save us. I've been calling for someone for so long, but no one hears us."

Chase kept trudging ahead. "You're the voice that people have heard in the woods?"

"Yes, whenever Dad fell asleep, Jenny stood guard, and I ran as fast as I could to the edge of the forest to call for help. No one ever came until today."

He glanced back. "Why did you ask for Sophia?"

The girl stepped up her pace. "Mom mentioned a woman named Sophia one time. She said we were related."

"Did your mother tell you how you were related?"

"She didn't. I called that name because it was the only name I knew."

Chase stopped for a moment to catch his breath. "How long have you been living here?"

"Almost two years after our mother died in a car crash. Dad said we had to get away from where we were living because some bad people were coming after us."

Chase finally reached the shoreline where an EMT was waiting for them.

"We'll take it from here," the woman said.

"This is her sister, Eleanor, and the girl's name is Jenny."

Chase crawled into the back of the ambulance with the girls, and he heard the EMT say they were taking them to the Logan Health Center in Kalispell. They arrived twenty minutes later, the emergency team whisking Jenny to the emergency room.

Chase sat out in the waiting room with Eleanor. An hour later the sheriff joined them. "Any word?" he asked.

Chase shook his head. "We're still waiting. What about Gene?"

The sheriff wiped his brow. "He's in a holding cell right now waiting for questioning. I wanted to see how the little girl was doing."

A doctor walked out to join them. "The little girl is going to make it just fine. We extracted the bullet, which came out clean. There won't be any long-standing issues. What about the parents?"

The sheriff answered. "We've called social services. Their mother has passed on, and we arrested their father."

"Gene is not our father," Eleanor said.

"We'll get it straightened out," the sheriff said.

Several moments later an older woman walked in. "Sheriff Portal, is this the young lady you've told me about?"

"Yes, this is Eleanor Clinton. Her sister is in the hospital with a leg wound."

"Eleanor, my name is Aubrey Dammond, and I will help you and your sister. Do you have any relatives?"

"My grandparents live in Helena."

Aubrey smiled. "That's wonderful, sweetheart. We'll contact them as soon as we can, but tonight, we'll put you with a temporary foster family until we can bring you to your grandparents."

"What about my sister?"

"She will be with you as soon as she can. Right now, let's get you settled."

Chapter 19

Once the social worker and Eleanor drove away, the sheriff turned to Chase. "I'll drive you back to Edgar's. Another crazy day in the county. I really don't know what to think about you being in Flathead. On the one hand you've made my life busier than normal, but on the other hand, you've helped us solve some mysteries that have been brewing for several years. Are you a mystery magnet or something?"

Chase laughed. "No, Sheriff, I just learn a lot from reading. I don't hope to come across issues like today. Speaking of today, the young girl told me that her mother mentioned the name Sophia one time. Most likely it's another Sophia, but what if those two girls are Nathan's girls and Gene was trying to protect them from him?"

Sheriff Portal's mouth dropped. "Nathan Shepherd has done some vile things in his life, and it wouldn't surprise me he's fathered other children. See what I mean? It's one thing after another with you."

Chase grinned. "Keeps you on your toes."

"On another note, Myra Kent is awake and she's going to make it. The doctor asked me to wait a little longer before talking to her."

"That's good news."

"It is. Do you feel like joining me for lunch?"

"I'll meet you at the bar and grill."

The sheriff turned onto the path to Edgar's cabin, stopped, and Chase climbed out. "I'll see you there, although it's 1:30, and it might be too late for lunch."

Chase slipped into his car, then followed the sheriff back to Mountain Ridge. They arrived thirty minutes later at the bar and grill. They entered to the blare of loud music. There were still people in the bar and grill eating and talking.

"Wow, at almost two the place is still full," Chase said.

"It's always like this. Isn't that Sophia sitting over there?"

Chase turned to where he pointed. Sophia wasn't alone.

"It looks like she's found another man in her life, but then she is probably one of the most beautiful women in Montana, so men gravitate toward her."

"It looks like it," Chase said. The two were chatting and laughing. For some reason he felt a pang in the pit of his stomach, something that he'd never experienced before. "Should we find a place to sit?"

They chose a small table by the window, and Jake came over with menus. "You two together doesn't bode well for the criminals in Flathead County." He grinned at them.

"What is that supposed to mean?" Sheriff Portal asked.

"Anytime you two are together, there's something happening in the county. What is it today?"

The sheriff frowned. "It's none of your business. What's the special?"

Jake laughed. "The Sheriff Portal we all love in fine form. Today's special is macaroni and cheese. Do you want that or the menu?"

They both chose the special. Once Jake left, Chase took another look at Sophia. "Why hasn't Sophia Shepherd married?"

The sheriff's eyes widened. "That's a strange question to ask."

He shrugged. "It is. Forget I even asked for it."

The sheriff leaned forward. "There are a couple of things about Sophia Shepherd you should keep in mind. First, she's a beautiful woman and every man is interested in her, so she guards herself closely. Second, she's a Shepherd, and that causes problems in itself— either good or bad. Many people believe the Shepherd family are crooks, but there are so many more who believe they are close to gods in this county. Sounds like anyone you know?"

"Are you talking about me by any chance?"

The sheriff nodded. "Just over the past few months, we've gotten to know each other better, and I've seen how hard it's been for you being a Connor. Just recently you lost a woman you had planned on marrying through no fault of your own. It was just too much pressure for Allison. Sophia goes through the same thing."

Their lunch arrived. Once Jake left, the sheriff continued, "Sophia remembers what you've done for her, especially after her manager was killed. You two have a chemistry that's hard to explain, but you choose to shy away from it."

Chase nodded as he ate his macaroni and cheese. Once finished, he spoke. "How can I put anyone else through what Allison had to go through? How can I expect either of them to deal with the name Connor? *I* have a hard time with it."

Sheriff Portal put down his fork. "I may have told you this once before, but some people are just made for each other, and Sophia and you are made for each other. I usually don't say things like this, but I'll break that vow this one time. As you know the Shepherds have plenty of insiders in the sheriff's department. Willis has told my deputies several times that the first question that has come out of Sophia's mouth over the last few months is 'how is Chase doing?'"

Chase rolled his eyes. "Why would he tell a deputy that?"

The sheriff smiled. "One of my deputies has had feelings for Sophia for several years."

"Willis always was a jerk, and this proves it by rubbing it into a guy who wants to be with her."

The sheriff finished his macaroni and cheese. "That's a Shepherd."

A voice came from above. "Are you ever going to stop badmouthing the Shepherds?"

Chase and the sheriff glanced up at Sophia who stood next to them with a man who had black hair, glasses, and wore a suit and tie.

The sheriff growled, "Caught me once more. Who do we have here?"

"Chase Connor, it's great to see you again."

"Toby Holland, it's been a while."

The sheriff peered over at Chase. "Why didn't you tell me you knew this guy?"

"No need to. He was with Sophia."

Sophia jumped in. "He just wanted to say 'hi' to you, Chase. Also, tomorrow night my parents are having a social event, and they would like you to attend."

Chase finished his water. "Tell them thank you, but I have things to do."

Toby interrupted. "Chase, that's not like you. You've always enjoyed rubbing shoulders with the elite, and the Shepherds are as elite as they are here. Besides, we have a lot to catch up on. "

"I'll think about it."

Toby smiled. "That's good enough."

Sophia jumped in. "Mr. Holland, we have a couple of more places to check out this afternoon."

"I told you to call me Toby. That's my name."

Sophia smiled and then glanced over at Chase. "I'll see you around. And Sheriff, I didn't hear a word you said about my folks. Have a wonderful day."

"You too, Sophia."

After they left, Sheriff Portal smirked. "He's a handsome man."

After they finished lunch, Chase went back to the bookstore and settled in for the afternoon. Along with thinking about Sophia, his mind focused on the mystery hunt. He searched for books around the bookstore that might have something to do with the subject. The only place he could find anything was in the mystery book, and it was vague.

Thinking about it all afternoon, he finally decided what he was going to do. He closed the bookstore at five, then climbed into the Jeep, and drove toward Mount Stimson which he knew was the highest elevation in Flathead County. The mountain reached more than 10,000 feet.

His first stop would be Whitefish where he would talk to Leah Furness to see if he could pull any more information out of her. Besides, he needed something to eat. He arrived in Whitefish close to six, parked the Jeep, and headed inside.

Leah was behind the bar. Good. He found a seat close to where she stood.

She peered up and noticed him. "What can I get you?"

"What do you have to eat?"

"Pizza, hamburgers, hot dogs—what would you like?"

"I'll go with the hamburger and fries, along with a beer."

She smiled. "Coming right up."

Once she placed the order, she joined him. "What brings you up here? I get off in another thirty minutes, so we can spend some time together." She waggled her eyebrows.

He grinned. "That's why I stopped by, but it's not what you were hoping for."

She frowned. "Okay, what do you have?"

"I wanted to talk to you about this mystery hunt and even take a ride to Mount Stimson."

She lifted her eyebrows. "Why the mountain?"

"The mystery hunt is in the highest elevation in the county, and I was hoping I could figure something out to help the sheriff."

She took a deep breath. "Believe me, you don't want to get involved with what's happening up there."

"Will you help me or not?"

Leah searched the room. "If we get caught up there, nothing good is going to come out of it."

"So, is that a yes?"

Leah laughed. "Yeah, I'm off in a half an hour, so I'll go with you. I'll let you finish your dinner."

Chapter 20

As they drove toward Mount Stimson, Leah pointed at various features around them. "The mountain is noted for its isolation, and it's one of the farthest peaks from a road in Glacier National Park. Are you sure you want to do this?"

"Yeah, something is happening up there, and I want to find out."

She sighed. "Chase, you should leave this for the sheriff's department. Nothing good is going to come out of it."

Chase didn't say anything but continued driving. Finally, he reached as far as he could before the road ended.

"Mount Stimson is still a couple of miles ahead," Leah said.

"Is that a creek or river ahead of us?"

Leah leaned forward. "That's Nyack Creek. There is a backpacking trail that runs along the creek, but there are National Park Service warnings that state it's brushier and more isolated than any other area of the park. Add to that numerous unabridged stream crossings and grizzly bears. Maybe it would be better to go through here when there's more daylight."

"Maybe you're right." Chase stared up the mountain. "I can see why it would be hard for anyone to find this place."

They drove back to Whitefish, and he parked in front of the bar.

Leah sat in the car. "Would you like to join me?"

He glanced at her. "Leah, you are a pretty woman, but I'm not the man you're looking for."

She laughed. "I don't want a long-term relationship, but you're a handsome man, and it would be amazing to spend a night with you."

Chase shook his head. "That's not me."

Leah peered at him. "There's someone you want to be with, but you're holding back for different reasons."

"How would you know that?"

"The name Connor is one reason." She opened the door. "A woman's advice—don't wait too long for her. She may find someone else, and you'll be the one left behind."

After she left, Chase drove toward Mountain Ridge. Leah was right about him holding back being with Sophia. One reason, of course, was being a Connor, but he was also afraid that he would get her into a situation that would end badly for her, and he didn't want that.

Here he was searching for a mountain path to help the sheriff solve a mystery, he could have been shot today, and several days ago he'd encountered the bear. Sophia had been right by his side. He would never forgive himself if something happened to her.

~

It had been a long day for Sophia. It was eight and

she was finishing the paperwork for her first house sale—actually, a cabin near Smith Lake. She'd spent much of the day with Toby Holland searching for the right building complex for their technology business.

Toby was a sweet man, handsome, and if Sophia wasn't so in love with Chase, he may be a man she would think about settling down with. They would be searching again tomorrow for property. There were a couple of sites she had arranged to view for later tomorrow morning.

As she finished her paperwork, Sophia turned out the lights of the office, then she stepped out onto Main Street. How beautiful a night it was this time of year. She unlocked the car door and started to climb in when a strong hand grabbed her arm. "Let me go," she said.

"I don't want to hurt you. I just want to talk to you." She peered up to see a masked face.

He released her arm.

"What do you want?" she asked.

"Please tell Chase Connor his life is in danger."

"Who are you?"

"Tell him the mystery man needs to stay away from the mountain."

"Why are you telling me this?"

"He listens to you."

Just like that the man whipped around and disappeared into the dark. Sophia leaned against her car trying to slow her heart down. Who was the guy? What was happening?

Instead of going home, she needed to see Chase. She locked the car then hurried down the street to the bookstore and rang the buzzer. No answer. Sticking the key into the lock, she opened the door, locked it, and went up the stairs. No Chase.

She grabbed a beer from his fridge and dropped onto the couch. After opening the drink, she took a long taste, set it down on the coffee table, then kicked off her shoes. Despite what had happened, she felt safe right here. Even better if Chase were holding her. She wanted to know so much more about him, but he wouldn't let her in. Maybe she needed to be more open about herself.

The door opened below, then she heard footsteps up the stairs, finally the apartment door opened. She cast her eyes on Chase.

"What are you doing here?"

For some reason she couldn't speak; she just trembled.

He hurried over to her, sat down by her, and wrapped his arm around her shoulders. "What happened?"

Sophia buried her head in his shoulder, and the tears came. Chase gently rubbed her head and spoke softly to her like he had done at least twice before.

She finally lifted her eyes. "Thank you."

"Are you calm enough to tell me what happened?"

"Some guy grabbed me and told me to tell you to stay away from the mountain. What did he mean?"

Chase stood up. "Do you want a beer?"

She shook her head. "I already have one. I just want you to talk to me."

Chase grabbed himself a beer, opened it, and took a drink. He sat back down next to her not saying anything.

Sophia peered into his eyes. "Thousands of guys watched me as I strutted down runways for almost ten years, but no eyes penetrated my heart as yours did when we first met each other in my family's backyard last fall. I fell in love with you at that moment, and I know you've fallen in love with me also, but for some reason you continue to shut me out. Why is that?"

When Chase didn't respond, Sophia continued. "I don't care if you're a Connor. I'm a Shepherd, and my family has done some rotten things to people, but they also have accomplished good things, much like your family has."

She grabbed her beer and took a swig, then she continued. "You're not like your family just like I'm not like my family. Heck, I'm working as a realtor, which I know nothing about, but I'm trying hard because I want to make it work for us. You could be a big-shot attorney, but you chose to purchase a bookstore, then an antique store, both which you've made something out of." She leaned her head back on the couch. "The most important issue here is that we've paved our own way in our lives, which is why we're nothing like our families. Our children will be doing the same thing when they grow up because neither of us will tell them to do this or do that." Sophia touched Chase's hand. "I don't even know when your birthday is."

He finally spoke. "It's August tenth. I'll be twenty-seven."

"Was that so hard? Mine is September first and I'll be the same age."

Chase sat back against the couch. "What you've said is true. When I sent Allison to my parents in California, I had no thoughts of asking her to marry me, but something happened, and we connected. I don't know if I truly loved her or if I felt sorry for her or if I was lonely. Maybe it was all of those and more."

Sophia waited for him to continue after he tasted his beer.

"She could have lost her life when I asked her to connect with a known drug dealer in order to put him away for good. In the end it wasn't she who could have died; it was me. The reason she left was she couldn't bear anything happening to me, and it was too much for her."

Sophia squeezed his hand. "You're assuming that if anyone is with you, something will happen to them."

"It's more than that."

"Then explain it to me."

He stood up. "I'm going to get another beer. Do you want one?"

"No, I'm good, but thank you."

Chase came back several minutes later with a beer and some chips. He sat back down next to her. She lifted his arm over her shoulders and squeezed close to him. "Go on."

He popped a chip into his mouth. "My family could have put Gartner away a long time ago, but they found ways to bend the law a bit and kept him out of jail. That's what we do. That's what I did for several years working as an attorney. A guy who died in prison a few months ago I'd gotten off twice before on some technicality, but it didn't change who he was."

Sophia grabbed one of the chips. "You wouldn't have known."

Chase frowned. "Yeah, I would have known since that was what always happened in our family. They are notorious for bending the law, and that's why the criminal element gravitates toward us."

She crawled onto her knees, leaned close to him, and framed his face with her hands. "That is not you. Maybe it was you at one time, but you are a guy who sells books and antiques, and also finds a way to help the sheriff out at times."

Chase drained his beer. "I'm not here to run a bookstore or antique store; I'm here to make amends for my past, so I do whatever I can to make sure that the right people are sent to prison, even if it means putting my life on the line. That's why you and I can never be together."

She reached over and kissed him gently on the lips, then slid back down into his arms. "I became a model for several reasons. One was to get as far away from my parents as I could. Another was to be this hotshot lady who strutted her stuff down the runway so everyone could see—maybe even hook up with some hot guy. I told myself I would never come back here, but I needed a break, and came back to see my parents last fall. Once I saw you, I had no problem staying in Montana because I hoped that you would be with me. Although it's been hard at the start, it'll happen."

He shook his head.

She peered deep into his eyes. "It can and it will. You realize that you're a multi-billionaire and you can do whatever you want, but you choose to live this life. You probably haven't touched any of your billions to make these two businesses successful. Does that sound like a Connor purchasing a bookstore and an antique store?"

Chase laughed. "It would never happen."

"But you've done it. I came back here because

every day I think about you, and every night before I fall asleep, I dream about the two of us together in each other's arms, our children jumping on our bed in a cabin in the Montana mountains."

His eyes went wide. "Six children?"

She grinned. "Maybe an exaggeration, but believe me, if it happened, I wouldn't be surprised. Once you let me into your life, we'll spend our nights in each other's arms. That will be a perfect world for me."

He pulled her near him and kissed her gently on the lips. She lifted her head to him. "Please don't do that to me unless you're prepared to go all the way."

Chapter 21

Chase's eyes popped open the next morning to the aroma of pancakes. He climbed off the couch and walked over to Sophia who was flipping a pancake. "Good morning," he said. "Did you sleep well?"

She grinned. "Silly question. I've told you before, when I'm in your arms it's perfect. Did you sleep well?"

"I did. Thanks for listening to me."

She pivoted and wrapped her hands around his neck. "Please continue opening up to me. Right now, you're not ready for a deep relationship, but you will be. I'll wait as long as I have to. Right now, breakfast is ready."

They sat down to eat. "Are you going to make this a habit every morning?"

"Sleeping with you or cooking breakfast?"

"Cooking breakfast."

"It would be much easier if we were sleeping together, but I'm okay with it. Of course, it won't happen every day because I have other commitments. By the way, I have a realtor conference in Denver in September. Would you go with me?"

"When and how long?"

"It starts on a Thursday and ends on a Sunday."

He swallowed the bite in his mouth. "I'm sure I can arrange it."

She smiled then stood. "Good. I'll see you tonight?"

"You're stopping by?"

She kissed him. "A social at my family's house, which you are specifically invited to."

"How can I forget?"

"Such an attitude is not good for a solid businessman. I love you, but now I have to go."

Once she left, Chase finished his pancakes. Sophia was a wonderful cook. He could get used to this. He shook his head. There was a long road ahead before anything like that would happen. He cleaned up the dishes and headed downstairs to open the bookstore.

It was a busy day for Chase, but Fridays were like that, since people would stop in to buy new books for the weekend. It was after five when a young man walked in with purple hair, half a mustache, and broken glasses.

"Can I help you?" Chase asked.

The man trembled. "Did the pretty woman talk to you about the mountain?"

Chase frowned. "Were you the guy who grabbed her?"

His hands visibly shook. "I didn't mean to hurt her; I just wanted her to tell you about the mountain."

"Why are you here?"

"I need to talk about what happens in that mountain to someone. People have said that you are the mystery book man and will listen to what I say without judgment."

"Maybe we should talk to the sheriff?"

He shook his head vehemently. "No law enforcement. They already have it in for me."

Chase motioned toward the back of the store. "How about we grab some coffee, have a seat, and talk?"

"Would you do that with me?"

"Sure. Join me in the break room."

The two walked into the room which was in the back of the bookstore. After Chase poured him the coffee, they sat down. Chase dropped a packet of sugar in his coffee and offered one to the man. "Let's start with who you are."

The man declined the sugar. "My name is Robert Tempest, and I live in the mountains near Creston. I've lived there by myself for the past five years, and I have seen and heard the weirdest things over those five years."

The man was extremely nervous, but perhaps he was just scared and telling the truth. He scratched his dirty long, purple hair, and continued. "The mystery hunt is not what it's supposed to be. They have this big idea about a group of people going up to this mountain hideaway, having a weekend-outdoor experience, but it doesn't happen."

"How would you know that?"

"I helped set it up in the past, but now they don't need me."

"Why don't they need you?"

He ran his fingers through his hair once more. "I saw some things I shouldn't have seen and ran. They didn't know I saw it, but it wasn't what was supposed to happen."

Chase took a drink and set down his mug. "What did you see?"

"For sure a lot of drugs and alcohol, but there were also women involved who were sexually active, if you know what I mean."

"Hookers?"

Robert nodded. "They weren't with the guests, but they were with a group of older men who seemed to have money."

"Did you see anybody you knew?"

Robert nodded. "Many people. The mayor, one of the county commissioners, even the district attorney was there one time, although he didn't do much with his woman."

Chase sipped some more coffee. "What does any of this have to do with the mystery hunt?"

"I'm getting to it. These big shots determine who will be involved with the weekend experience, plus they also assign those who will be with the guests over the weekend. The problem is no one knows who these people are because they're always dressed differently and wear masks."

"Do the guests wear masks?"

He nodded as he took a sip of his drink. "There is a pickup and drop-off point. It changes every year, and no one knows the person who's behind this mystery hunt. Masks must be worn at all times outside the cabins, but once inside, anything's fair game."

Chase stirred his coffee. "Do you know who Myra Kent is?"

Robert thought for a moment then nodded. "She was one of the guests for the most recent mystery hunt. Rumor has it that she and the man she was with heard some noises at night and took off scared."

"Has that happened before?"

"That's the first time that happened, but who knows what went on inside their cabin. You don't believe me, do you?"

Chase took a deep breath. "Honestly, it does seem strange, but I've also read about and dealt with weird things since I've been here. Is there a way to get to those cabins?"

"They're guarded at all times because it's private property."

"Do you know who owns the property?"

Robert sneezed, then stared at Chase. "I don't."

Chase sighed. "It's simple enough to find out who owns the deed at the courthouse."

"Good luck," Robert said, "Others have tried and struck out."

Chase's eyes popped at the text that came over his phone. "Shoot," he said out loud, reading the text from Sophia.

"Is everything okay?"

Chase nodded. "I was supposed to be somewhere an hour ago."

"I'm sorry I took up so much of your time, but I thought this was important to tell you. Like I said, I couldn't tell law enforcement since I don't know who to trust."

Chase glanced at Robert. "I'll drive out to your cabin late tomorrow morning, so you can show me where the place is located. Are you okay with that?"

"Better yet, I'll meet you out there right after lunch."

"Sounds good."

He nodded. "I should go so you can get to your meeting."

Chapter 22

Robert Tempest stepped outside the bookstore, buttoned his jacket, and hurried down the block, then around the corner. In front of him stood a man a few inches taller than he.

"Did you relay the information to Connor?"

"I did."

"Do you think he believes it?"

Robert sighed. "I'm not sure, but he did say he has run across weird things since he's been in Montana and he's going to meet me at the cabin late tomorrow morning."

"That's perfect. You did your job."

The two headed toward a black car. "Hop in, Robert, and we'll give you a ride back to your cabin."

"Thanks for the lift up and back. It seems like this is very important. I'm glad you let me be part of it."

The man grinned. "Your part is about over. Let's go for a ride."

Robert hopped into the car, and they drove toward Creston, then Mount Stimson. Thirty minutes later they arrived at the cabin, and Robert stepped out.

Standing there were four men with rifles. Robert

whipped around to the guy in the car. "What is this?"

"You have about two minutes to start, then they'll be hunting you down. You wanted to be part of the mystery hunt, so now's your chance."

"But, sir, I did as you asked."

"A minute and fifty seconds."

Robert turned and started running as fast as he could toward the cabin. It was up a steep mountain, and he could hear the men behind whistling and shouting his name. It was just like what happened to the woman and her boyfriend at the June mystery hunt.

He made it up to the cabin, tried to get inside, but it was locked. Shaking, he turned to see the four men, their rifles aimed at him. He hurried around the right side of the cabin to a trail he knew about. He stumbled up the mountain.

"Robert Tempest, we're getting closer. You're about to meet your maker."

Sweat dropped down his face as he continued climbing up the mountain trail, falling at times, turning to see where they were. One was close enough he could see the rifle pointed at him. He jumped up and continued climbing as fast as he could.

When he reached the top of the mountain, Robert searched for somewhere else to go. He was trapped. Whipping around, he saw the four men with rifles pointed at him once more. "Please, don't do this to me. I don't know anything about what is happening."

The four stepped back as a man silhouetted in the moonlight stepped up. "Robert, you've seen way too much, which means you can't live any longer, but if it's any consolation, the last thing you'll know is that you were the one who helped end Chase Connor's life."

The man stepped back as the four men shot at once. Robert screamed as he fell backwards, hurtling off the mountain.

~

The man stood over the edge and stared down at Robert as he bounced off a couple of rocks. He turned back to the four men. "Make sure his body isn't found."

One of the men spoke. "Yes, sir. We'll take care of it. What next?"

The silhouetted man took a deep breath. "He did his job. Chase Connor is next."

~

Chase hurried into the Shepherds' house trying to tie his tie. What a mess! But then he never could figure out the blasted thing. He ran into Penelope.

"Chase Connor, you seem to be frustrated."

"Yeah, I can't figure out this tie."

"Here let me see it," she said. Her fingers looped the ends, then she pulled it up for him. "There you go. You're a handsome man dressed up."

Chase smiled. "Thanks, Penelope, and you look nice in your strapless dress."

She blushed. "Too much makeup, but Glen Allan loves me looking like this."

"I'm sure he does. I should find the bar because I know I'm going to need a drink."

Penelope pointed. "Right over there."

"Thanks. By the way, where's Glen Allan?"

"He's schmoozing with the Shepherds and the technological gurus. They're right over there."

Chase turned to where she was pointing and saw Sophia with them. She looked adorable, dressed in her turquoise short dress, with boots, and her hair done just perfectly.

"Sophia Shepherd is a beautiful woman," Penelope said. "You should be with her."

"She's with someone who's much more respectable than me." Chase strolled over to the bar, grabbed himself a glass of wine, and some hors d'oeuvres. He needed plenty of both tonight since he wasn't sure what was happening. He turned to a woman's voice.

"Chase Connor, I'm surprised you would show up to our house after what you did to my husband and son."

"Mrs. Shepherd, you look nice tonight."

"Don't try to butter me up, young man. When are you going to stop chasing after my family? You have no right to do such things after all the things you and your family have done over the years, but then you're a Connor, so it shouldn't surprise me."

"Mrs. Shepherd, I have no clue why I'm here, other than Mr. Holland invited me."

Toby Holland joined them. "Chase, I'm glad you could make it. Mrs. Shepherd, thanks for keeping Chase company until we got here."

Mrs. Shepherd lifted her chin and hurried away.

Toby laughed. "See you have a way with women."

"It seems that way."

"Mom and Dad have been waiting to see you. This way."

Chase followed Toby over to his parents who were with Nathan, Willis, and Sophia. "Oh my, Chase, you have changed so much," Mrs. Holland said. She reached over and kissed him on the cheek. "I've wanted to do that for so long."

Mr. Holland laughed. "She has. How have you been?" He said, shaking his hand. "When Toby said you were here, I couldn't believe it. It makes it so much easier to do business here knowing that there is someone here we can trust." He turned to Nathan and Willis. "Meaning no disrespect, but Chase and Toby go way back. You may not have known that Toby and Chase's brother, Micah, were in the same class at Stanford, but it was Chase who was the top of the class when he went through."

Mrs. Holland grinned. "Now you run a bookstore and antique shop. How the mighty have fallen."

Chase grinned right back. "You're right, but I'm okay with that. It's an honest day's work." Chase turned to the Shepherds. "Nathan, Willis."

They nodded at him. Chase touched Sophia's hand. "You look nice," he said softly.

"And so do you."

Mr. Holland jumped in. "No wonder Toby can't get anywhere with this beauty. You have her all wrapped up."

Chase offered a weak smile. "No, Mr. Holland, her parents wouldn't be too happy with me being part of their lives."

"You're right there," Willis said.

"Willis, calm down," Nathan said. "Remember, Chase Connor is still a guest in our house, and tonight he may be the most important guest."

"Toby invited me, but I have no idea about anything that this group is doing."

Mr. Holland sipped his wine. "Then let me enlighten you. Holland Technology is expanding, and we want to move a major portion of our company to

Mountain Ridge. Ms. Shepherd has been so kind to show Toby several places, and we believe we've found the perfect spot, but we want you to check everything out to make sure it'll work."

"Mr. Holland, I'm not an attorney anymore."

Toby jumped in. "We all know that, but you're still the person we trust to make this work."

Chase took a drink from a caterer who passed. "I'm sorry Toby, but it can't be me. I wouldn't be objective, since you're working with the Shepherds."

Mr. Holland jumped in. "We know the backstory of what happened, and we're not necessarily working with the Shepherds, but they do have influence in this county, and it's important that we have a connection with them. You understand how that works."

Chase peered at Mr. Holland. "I do, and that's why I won't be part of it. Sorry."

Sophia took his arm. "Let me talk to Chase," she said to Mr. Holland. The two walked to another part of the room. "What are you doing?" Sophia said.

"I won't have anything to do with your family."

She took a deep breath. "I know how you feel about my family, but this is legitimate, aboveboard with all involved. Please trust me."

He locked eyes with her. "What are you doing, Sophia?"

"What do you mean?"

"All of a sudden, you're this power broker when last night you were happy being a realtor."

"I haven't changed who I am, but I also realize that in order for Mountain Ridge to grow, companies need to come in or expand, and that's what's happening here. You're the one who told me that the Hollands were a solid group. Do you believe they would sully that reputation?"

"No, you're right, but they could find someone else to check everything out."

Sophia sipped her wine.

He laughed. "You asked them to do this? Why would you do that?"

"I know you, Chase Connor, and you'll do anything you can to make sure it's a fair deal all the way around."

"What do you get out of it?"

"Nothing, other than knowing the man I love is doing one more thing that helps the community. You've done that with the bookstore and the antique store. This is a major technology company. If nothing else, please do it for me."

His eyes glared at her. "You're asking way too much! My family did that to me all the time."

Chapter 23

Sophia could feel her throat tighten knowing she had screwed up royally, but she also discovered one more layer to the man. She would remember never to do anything like that again.

"What did Chase say?" Toby asked.

"It's a big 'no.'"

"That's too bad," Toby said, "because I'm not sure if my parents will expand here without his say so."

Sophia peered up. "Why would it matter what Chase has to say?"

Toby took her hand. "Let's get out of here to talk."

They headed out into the backyard and sat down on a bench. Toby scooted closer to Sophia than she had wanted, so she discreetly moved over a bit.

"Now what is it about Chase that is important to your family?"

Toby swilled his drink. "Do you know Peter Drake?"

Sophia shook her head. "Chase has never mentioned him."

He didn't answer right away. It was as if he were choosing his words.

"Drake used to work for Chase's father at the law firm. He wasn't an attorney, but Peter worked in buying property for different types of businesses—resorts, large-scale buildings, you name it. Anyway, a couple of years ago, Peter and Oliver Connor got into an argument over some property in southern Idaho that Connor wanted to purchase, but Peter said he wouldn't deal with it because of the Native Americans who were living on the property.

Toby took a glass of wine from the platter as the caterer passed. "Connor fired Peter but also sent his son, Micah, and a man named Hamilton after him. Hamilton is a known killer for the Connor family. He goes after undesirables, people who screw the Connor family over, and whoever Oliver Connor tells him to get rid of. Connor was so ticked at Peter he sent Hamilton and Micah after him."

"Did they kill him?" Sophia asked, her eyes wide.

"Nope, Chase saved Peter's life. Always remember, if you see Micah Connor and Hamilton together, someone is going to die. Chase stepped in and they backed down."

Sophia sighed. "Why would they back down to Chase? He's their youngest brother."

"Yeah, but he has the majority of the money."

"Okay, Chase is a billionaire like the rest, so why would it matter?"

"Sophia, you really don't know who Chase Connor is. The Connor estate totals more than $55 billion dollars. Chase's portion is more than $30 billion dollars, meaning he has the majority share of their stock. His grandfather gave it to Chase in his will, so the rest of the family does everything they can to protect him because if something happens to Chase Connor, every penny of his money goes into a foundation they won't be able to touch."

Sophia didn't respond. How could she? *There's so much I don't know about Chase.*

Toby reached over to kiss Sophia, but she lifted her hand for him to stop. "I'm in love with Chase."

"Then he's a very lucky man."

"No, I'm a lucky woman. I modeled for almost ten years, and had thousands of men hit on me, but he's the only one who makes me feel like a woman. Until he gets past this Connor complex, we'll be stuck in limbo, but I'll wait as long as it takes."

They both turned to a voice behind them. "There you two are." Sophia's father was hurrying toward them.

"Dad, what's wrong?" Sophia asked, sensing something was off-kilter.

"Nothing, now," he smiled. "I'm glad the two of you are finding some time alone together."

"Don't go there." Sophia stood up. "Thanks, Toby, for the talk. Good night, and we'll meet tomorrow at ten-thirty at the property you checked out."

"Where are you going?" Toby asked.

She grinned. "I'm going to convince Chase he should help out. By the way, who is Peter Drake to you?"

Toby sighed. "He's my mother's brother."

It was past nine-thirty when Sophia pressed the button for Chase's apartment. He responded after a couple of buzzes. "What do you want now?"

"Please, Chase, let me up?"

"Go home."

She laughed. "I can always just use a key and come upstairs myself."

Chase buzzed her in. She stepped in and walked upstairs. Chase was sitting on the couch in shorts and a t-shirt watching television when she opened the door to his apartment. She plopped down next to him. "Well, what show are you watching on one of your three channels?"

Chase rolled his eyes. "Nothing really, but I should change the lock on the bookstore door."

She leaned into him. "And miss these opportunities for stimulating conversation?"

Despite what had happened, Chase spewed out a laugh. "Why are you here?"

She linked her arms with his. "First, I want to say I'm sorry about using myself or for that matter, you, as a means to an end. I should have known better. Second, why didn't you tell me you were a multi-billionaire?"

"What are you talking about?" he said, looking over at her.

"You're worth more than $30 billion dollars and you never said one word to me about it."

"I've never said one word to anyone about it. It's no one's business, and besides I don't use it anyway, so it can go wherever."

Sophia stared into his eyes. "You didn't know if something happens to you all the money goes into foundations?"

Chase chortled. "That makes total sense now. My family will do whatever they can to have a piece of the pie. What does any of this have to do with the Hollands?"

Sophia stood. "I need a drink. Would you like

something?"

"Some lemonade."

Her eyes lit up. "When did you start drinking lemonade?"

"Tonight, after I made it."

She giggled, went into the kitchen, poured two glasses of lemonade, and rejoined him. She handed him a glass, then sipped hers. "Wow, this tastes good. I'll have to change my drink when I come over here. Back to the story. You stopped your brother and this Hamilton character from taking care of Peter Drake. Why did you do that?"

"Simple, Peter Drake didn't do anything but tell the truth, but then my dad was always bullheaded thinking he knew everything. Peter Drake was right about the property. So what?"

"Did you know Peter Drake is Mrs. Holland's brother?"

Chase set his drink down, his voice low. "I didn't know that."

"That's why they want your help. They trust you to help them make the right decision. I don't know what angle my father has in all of this, but I do know just from the short time I've been with the Hollands that they're sincere people and want to do the right thing."

"They are."

"Then help them. We're trying to change our lives from the past, and this is another chance. I'll be right there with you, or if you decide not to, I'll support you. I just want you to do what you feel is right."

He shifted his glance to her. "Did Toby try to kiss you?"

"What?" Sophia said, her face warming.

"Wow, he did. Did you respond?"

Her expression changed to a glare. "Of course I didn't. Like I told him, you're the man I love, and I'll wait as long as it takes."

"Then I'll help him."

What? She backed up. "Because I didn't kiss him?"

"No, because you care about how I feel."

She kissed him, then laid her head on his chest. "Right answer, and I always will."

Chapter 24

After Sophia ate breakfast with Chase, she started to head out the door, but stopped and hurried back. "I almost forgot," she said, kissing him solidly on the lips. "Much better this morning."

Chase laughed.

Sophia grinned. "I'll see you at the office around ten-thirty. I love you."

Chase watched as she hurried out the door. If nothing else, Sophia was consistent. Every day for the last week, she had spent the night on the couch with him, cooked him breakfast, then hurried out the door to her house to change clothes. He'd have to ask her how her family was taking all of this. Maybe he'd even suggest she leave some clothes at the apartment, but then she might want to move in with him.

He finished what he needed to do, then headed down the street to the realty company. When he walked in, he saw two other people waiting in the lobby. Sophia was taking care of another person while the others were waiting for her.

An older lady with white hair in curlers peered up at him. "Chase Connor, how have you been?"

He sat down in a chair two seats from her. "Mrs.

Jorg, you're looking for a place to live?"

"Nope, I hope to sell my cabin in the mountains."

"I didn't know you had a cabin. I've only picked you up in town."

She nodded as she sipped her coffee. "When my husband passed, I moved into the city limits. It was too much out there. Too many parties in the vicinity, weird happenings all the time."

"Where's your cabin located?"

"Near Mount Stimson."

The name immediately got his attention. "How close is Mount Stimson?"

"If you call a third of the way up the mountain close, then that's it. Are you interested?"

This was like a gift. "I actually am. Can you give me the directions or address, and I'll check it out?"

She gave him the address. Sophia strolled over to her. "I'm ready for you, Mrs. Jorg."

"This handsome man is interested in my cabin, so I gave him the address. I'll see what happens after he looks at it then go from there."

"Okay," Sophia said, as the older lady stood to leave. Once she walked out the door, Sophia glanced at Chase. He just shrugged. Sophia turned to the other man waiting for her.

It was past eleven when Sophia and Chase left the realtor's office. He climbed into the passenger side of her car.

Once they headed out of the parking lot, she asked, "what was that all about?"

"What? The mountain house?"

"Yes, the mountain house."

"I'm just interested in it."

"Don't lie to me, Chase."

"How would you know I was lying?"

"Simple, the change in your voice."

"Wow, you noticed that?"

She giggled. "Yep, I do know a few things about you and am learning more. Now out with it."

"I'll tell you later. Where's Toby?"

"We're meeting him out there. He had some other business this morning." Sophia drove toward the south end of town, pulled into a large lot, and parked the car in front of a rough-looking building.

Chase turned to Sophia. "They're interested in this?"

"The city of Mountain Ridge is hoping to annex this into the city as commercial property. The total annexation would be ten acres. The Hollands would have six acres of it with the other four acres available if they wanted it. The cost for the six acres is 1.3 million dollars."

"Not a bad price, so what is the problem?"

"Infrastructure, but if the city annexes it, they'll help out with those costs."

"How close is the city to annexing the property?"

Sophia opened the door. "The city council will vote on it tomorrow. There is another company interested in the property also, or I should say, the other four acres."

Chase frowned. "Your father?"

She nodded. "I'm trying to talk Toby and his father into buying all ten acres." She leaned toward him. "I don't want my family to screw this up for the Hollands." She shut the door and Chase joined her. They walked into the building which featured a large atrium. Waiting for them were Mr. Holland, his son,

Toby, and Nathan and Willis Shepherd. Toby laughed. "When Sophia said she would get you here, she was right."

Chase didn't say anything. Sophia jumped in. "Let's take a look at what the building has to offer." Sophia pulled out building diagrams and handed them to all those present in the room. "Your thoughts on this large area that measures 100 by 200 feet?"

Mr. Holland studied the blueprint. "I believe this would be a perfect size, but it will need work to bring it up to snuff. What do you think, Toby?"

"I like it a lot. It's probably the best venue we've seen so far. Let's take a look at the rooms."

They quickly checked each room out, then headed to an office off the atrium. "It seems like rooms are all the same size except this office," Willis said.

Mr. Holland shrugged. "The larger room could house the computer equipment that will be needed to run the technology center." He turned to Chase. "Your thoughts?"

Chase glanced around the group then back to Mr. Holland. "First, explain what you hope to accomplish with this business."

Mr. Holland grinned. "Good question. Sophia asked that earlier. The primary focus at this facility will be research, development, and manufacture of technology-based goods and services."

Chase thought for a moment. "You could expand any of your businesses to fulfill that need. Why here?"

"Two key elements—lower costs and bringing new jobs to the Mountain Ridge area."

Chase frowned. "I can understand that, but wouldn't it benefit you to purchase all ten acres?"

"Why would you suggest that?" Nathan asked.

"Ten acres would be much better than six acres to turn this into a major technological complex out here in northern Montana. It could be a state-of-the-art small technology facility that other companies could visit and see how something like this can be done in a small community."

"It's something to think about," Mr. Holland said. "Anyone else have anything to add?"

Nathan Shepherd jumped in. "The annexation should be approved on Tuesday, but under the current proposal, this site is only listed at six acres, and the four acres are slated for another project."

Mr. Holland studied Nathan. "Do you know what that project is or who is spearheading it?"

"Not at this point."

Toby interrupted. "I was under the impression that you have a pulse on everything that happens in this county."

Nathan glared at the younger Holland. "At this point, I'm not sure."

Chase jumped in. "You can always check with the county planner to see what is happening with construction projects throughout the county."

Mr. Holland glanced over at Sophia. "I believe you've already done that."

Sophia flipped through a file on the desk. "There is a construction project being considered for the four acres for a small technology business."

Mr. Holland's eyes lit up. "Who else is interested in starting a technology business?"

Sophia's eyes slanted toward Chase and then back to Mr. Holland's. "Willis Shepherd."

Everyone turned to Willis. Mr. Holland glared at Nathan. "You knew about my plans for this property! How could you lie about this?"

He shrugged. "It's news to me."

Mr. Holland's eyes narrowed. "Explain to me why you would do something like this, knowing that my company is interested in this piece of property and expanding my technology business?"

Willis's face flushed. "I thought that I could add on to what you hope to accomplish with your research in technology and use my business as a start-up facility for those interested."

Toby frowned, then he turned to Sophia. "How would he know we're interested in this piece of property?"

Sophia lifted a shoulder. "He wouldn't, but this has been considered prime property for the last several months."

Sophia didn't like the way Toby Holland was glancing at her—Chase noticed it. He jumped in. "Mr. Holland, you asked me to come along to provide advice. Here it is— Either buy all ten acres and draw up a partnership with the Shepherds, or find another piece of property. Any way you look at it, Willis Shepherd won't be able to build his business without your help."

"Or we can just go somewhere else." Toby said.

Sophia huffed. "If you think I know anything about what my brother had in mind, then you can go find someone else to do business with. I'm not like my family; nor will I ever be like them." She stormed out of the facility.

Mr. Holland stepped in. "Toby, let's have a chat." He motioned for Chase to join them.

They moved out of the hearing range of the others. Nathan glared at his son. "Why didn't you tell me this was your plan?"

"Do I have to tell you everything?"

"Yes, you do, especially if it could ruin an opportunity for the family."

Willis groaned. "Not everything revolves around cars."

"You'll remember that the car dealership is what's put money in your pocket." He shifted toward Chase. "I'm surprised that you're even involved with Sophia after leaving her for Willis's girlfriend. But then you're a Connor, so it shouldn't surprise me."

Chase kept his mouth shut, not saying what he was thinking—that the Shepherds were criminals and should be sitting in jail. He followed the father and son back to the group.

"What have you decided, Mr. Holland?" Nathan asked.

"First of all, we both agree that your daughter knew nothing about what transpired with your son, Willis, but we will not do business with your son. If he's scheming something like this now, what will he do in the future?"

Nathan lifted a dismissive hand. "Willis understands the position he has put us in and is sorry about the whole affair."

Mr. Holland's expression remained hard to read. "Toby is adamant about finding another spot or moving this technological business to another location. I'm inclined to agree with him on this point, but we'll think about it overnight and give a final decision tomorrow morning. Please join us for breakfast tomorrow at the bar and grill."

Nathan and Willis strode out of the facility. Chase turned to the Hollands. "Thanks for realizing that Sophia knows nothing about it. She's not like her family. Sophia is aboveboard, and will do what's best for this community."

Toby sighed. "Yeah, I was wrong, and I must admit she is a lot like you. I actually tried to kiss her, but she abruptly stopped me and told me you were the only man who would ever kiss her. I'm going to tell Sophia how sorry I am. I'll see you outside, Dad."

After Toby left, it was just Mr. Holland and Chase. Mr. Holland shook his head. "I should have known better than to do business with the Shepherds. They're always working an angle, much like your father. The problem is I truly like this area, its beauty, the people—at least most of the people, and I believe this will be a wonderful opportunity."

"I fell in love right away with it also. Other than the blizzards—they suck."

Mr. Holland laughed. "I can imagine that. My wife will never forget what you did for her brother, so I'll ask you one last time—What do you think about all of this?"

Chase lifted a shoulder. "First of all, the Shepherds will stick their nose in everything, will possibly direct how the city annexes this property, and who knows what else. If it was my decision, I would make sure the Shepherds had nothing to do with your business. That means a conversation with the city council on how your business will make this a better community." He lifted his chin. "Buy all ten acres. One last thought, contact Mr. Grenham tonight. He has a major distribution company and is working with me on Native American studies, but he might also be willing to work with your technology company to help his cause. He's a powerful man who could help sway the city council your way."

"Mr. Grenham?" Mr. Holland asked.

"Right, you wouldn't know who he was. Mr. Grenham has a distribution network and is also working with me on a reading program for the bookstore and for the Flathead Reservation. Here's his information if you're interested."

Mr. Holland took the card and studied it.

Chase started for the door, but he stopped. "I'm sorry, but I have one last thing. This county has many quality leaders, but people like the Shepherds tear it down, so it's important not to associate with them if possible."

Mr. Holland eyed him. "All good points. My wife noticed the connection you and Ms. Shepherd have with each other. You'll always be a Connor and she'll always be a Shepherd, but you two can forge your own world if you just take a chance on her."

Chase shook his head. "I wish I could, but as you said, I'll always be a Connor."

Chapter 25

Chase and Mr. Holland walked out to the lot where Sophia and Toby were leaning against her car talking to each other. They both stopped and looked their way. They said something, then started laughing.

"I'm glad to see that they aren't going away mad at each other," Mr. Holland said.

"The same here. I hope things work out for your company. Like I said, the majority of people in this area are good people. Like California there are always those who try to get ahead any way they can."

"Thanks for your input," Mr. Holland said. "No matter what happens, I see a change in you. You've always been the one Connor people want to do business with, but in the last couple of days, I see a man who is maturing and has the world ahead of him. Always remember you need a good woman to be there with you when times get tough. Mrs. Holland has been a godsend for me. I wouldn't be where I am today without her."

They both turned at Toby's voice. "We have to go, Dad."

Mr. Holland headed to the car and peered at Sophia. "I'm sorry about all that has transpired today.

In business, you always run into people who don't play by the rules, but it's nice to know that there are still people who do the right thing, and more importantly, have their sights set on the community above others."

"Thanks, Mr. Holland. I'm positive that everything will turn out fine."

After the Hollands drove off, Chase wrapped his arm around Sophia. "I'm proud of the way you handled everything today. Pretty professional, if I do say so myself."

She snuggled close to his chest. "Thanks, I needed to hear that." She lifted her head and kissed him. "Thank you for supporting me in all of this. You didn't have to be here today."

He squeezed her shoulder. "Yeah, I had to."

"Why?"

"You've been there for me, so it was important that I be there for you."

Sophia lifted his arm off her. "Let's go get some lunch?"

"In Creston?"

Sophia eyed him. "Okay, it's Creston."

They climbed into the car and headed to a small cafe in the town near Mount Stimson. After Sophia pulled into a parking spot, they walked into the cafe and found a place to sit. The waitress came over with a menu.

Sophia slipped out of the booth and sat next to Chase. He rolled his eyes. She giggled. "Since we have one menu, we'll have to study it together."

They both decided on a soup and sandwich with iced tea. After the waitress took their orders, Sophia stayed next to Chase. "Why are we here?"

"Do you have any appointments this afternoon?"

"No, my day is pretty open, so what do you have in mind?"

He grinned. "How do you feel about looking at a cabin near here?"

She grinned back. "I know it's not for us, so what's going on?"

"You're right as usual. I'll tell you everything later. Right now, I need to check something out."

Sophia took Chase's hands. "Please, stop playing the hero. Even though we're not together, someday we will, and I need you in my life."

"I'm sorry, but it's something I have to do to try to clear all the things that I've done during my life."

Tears brimmed in her eyes. "You're only twenty-six. We've talked about how those things you did in your past are over with."

The waitress brought their food to them, and they ate quietly. Once finished, they climbed into Sophia's car and drove up to the cabin. She pulled in as far as she could go.

Chase turned to her. "I'll be back as soon as I can."

She opened the car door. "No, if you're going to play the hero, I'm going to be there right with you."

"You're in a skirt and boots."

She started walking up the mountain. "Are you coming with me?"

Chase grinned and followed her up the mountain. He caught up with her when they got closer to the cabin. "What are we actually looking for?" Sophia asked.

"We're meeting Robert Tempest, who is the guy who grabbed you in your car."

"Why would we do that?"

"He has some information about this mystery hunt, and I hope to find out something more today. He said this cabin is near where they hold that event."

They arrived at the cabin. Chase jumped onto the porch and knocked on the door. He knocked three times, but no one answered. He pushed the door, and it opened.

"What are you doing, Chase? You can't just break into someone's home."

"I thought I heard something in there, so if that's the case, we can go in to make sure there isn't anyone hurt."

Sophia grinned. "Who are you, a lawyer or a bookstore owner?"

"Depends on the day."

They entered and looked around. The cabin had a large living room space, a kitchen, and a fireplace. They walked back to the bedrooms. There was a master bedroom and two other bedrooms with two bathrooms.

"This would be a perfect starter home for a newly married couple or a family with just a couple of children," Sophia said.

He stopped and stared at her. She rolled her eyes. "I'm thinking like a realtor. I realize that I'll be in my forties before you finally decide you want to marry me."

They searched for a few more moments and saw nothing. "Let's take a look outside," Chase said. "He said he'd meet me up here."

They headed up the trail, stopped when it ended, and looked up at the mountain. Sophia tapped Chase on the shoulder. "What is that?"

They hurried over to where she was pointing. Chase bent down and found a torn shirt. He lifted his eyes. "It looks like the color of material from the man's jacket."

Sophia took it. "It sure does. What happened?"

"Could be anything, but I do know that there are bears up in this region."

"Everybody knows there are bears in Montana."

Chase, noting her sarcastic expression, rolled his eyes. "I drove up this way with the bartender at the Whitefish bar a couple of days ago to check out the area. She was telling me about what was around here."

Sophia didn't say anything, just listened.

"I know all of this bothers you, but something is happening to people in this area, and if I can help the sheriff find out what's happening, it's a good thing."

"I never said it wasn't a good thing. I'm just saying it doesn't have to be you running around the countryside. Call in the tips to the sheriff's department."

Chase took her into his arms and peered into her eyes. "Since Gartner, your father, and your brother were involved recently in the drug activities, the sheriff doesn't trust his deputies, and the public has no confidence in the sheriff's department, so I'm trying to do what I can."

The twinkle returned to her eyes. He kissed her, and she matched his passion. He stepped back. "I should have never done that."

"Yes, you should have. That's what I want you to do, that and more."

Something caught Chase's attention out of the corner of his eye.

"What?" Sophia turned to where he was looking.

"I thought I saw something or someone. Get back to the car and call the sheriff."

~

Sophia grabbed for Chase, but he went down another trail. She hurried back to the car, climbed in, and called the sheriff. He answered on the third ring. "Sheriff Portal, Chase asked me to call you and get you up near Mount Stimson."

"What has your boyfriend got himself into now?"

"I don't know, but he's not my boyfriend. Please hurry."

Once she got off her cell phone, she hurried back up the mountain toward Chase. She found the trail he had entered, then raced up it. Several minutes later she found Chase bent over staring at the ground. Someone or something was coming toward him.

She screamed. "Chase, behind you."

Chase rolled to his left as an ax landed next to him. He kicked out his legs, and his assailant fell backwards. The man jumped up and raced deep into the mountains.

Sophia slid down next to Chase. "Are you okay?"

He grinned. "Just a bit close."

She started pounding on his shoulder, tears flowing down her face. "He could have killed you. What were you thinking?"

Chase reached over, grabbed her arm, and pulled her near him. "Why did you come back?"

She stared into his eyes. "I told you I'd never leave you."

The two stared at each other, their breath coming in fits and starts. "Did you get a look at him?" Sophia asked.

Chase shook his head. "He had a mask on his face. But he did leave his weapon, and maybe the sheriff's department can get fingerprints."

Chase pushed to his feet, but Sophia pulled him back down. "What?"

She peered into his eyes. "Stop this nonsense. We love each other deeply, so please be with me forever."

He grinned. "Are you asking me to marry you?"

"I am, Chase. I'd wait forever for you to ask me to marry you, but that's too far from now. I'm going to take the initiative."

He stood up. "It doesn't work that way." He reached out his hand and he pulled her up.

"What does that mean exactly?" she asked.

"I'm a Connor."

He picked up the ax by the head and headed back toward the trail they'd veered off. She hurried after him. "Explain what that means—'I'm a Connor.'"

Chase didn't respond. She took his hand and the two walked down the trail. They were almost at the Jeep when the sheriff and a deputy started the climb up. "You missed all the fun," Chase said.

The sheriff stopped. "Did you knock down a tree or someone's skull?"

"I wish it would have been someone's skull," Chase said. "I brought the ax back because maybe you can lift the fingerprints off it. A guy in a mask decided he wanted to try to make firewood out of me."

Chapter 26

Sophia pulled in front of the bookstore to drop Chase off. She turned the ignition off and shifted to talk to Chase. "That man swinging that ax at you scared me, so I panicked. I do want to be your wife, but I know you're not ready. I'm sorry for pressuring you."

"Don't be sorry. Realize that I am terrified I will lose you because of something I've done, and that's the main reason we can't be together. After seeing how terrified you were, I've decided just to stick to books and antiques and leave the rest to the sheriff." He opened the door. "Good night, and I love you."

"I love you also."

Once Sophia left, Chase went upstairs, filled up his bottle with lemonade, and grabbed a jacket. His mind was running like crazy, so there was no hope for sleep any time soon. He walked back down the stairs, out the door, and an hour later he was sitting on a bench overlooking Smith Lake.

He needed to let Sophia in his life, he knew that. Chase needed to tell her everything that had haunted him since he was a little boy so she would understand why he was the way he was. He held his memories so deep he was afraid if he let it all out, there would be no more Sophia.

Before he could change his mind, he texted her to join him right now.

She responded almost right away that she would. For the next fifteen minutes until she showed up, he thought about what he was going to say.

A car pulled up, Sophia jumped out, and ran over to him. She slid down next to him. "Are you okay? Are you hurt?"

"I'm fine."

"Then why did you call me?"

He took her hands. "For the last hour, I've been trying to figure out how to tell you things about me—What's haunted me throughout my life."

She squeezed his hands. "Talk, I won't judge. I want to know."

He took a deep breath. "The life of a Connor is much different than the life of most other people. You have a nice house, but I lived in a castle on a hill overlooking the Pacific Ocean, so large you could get lost in it for days, and no one would know."

He tasted his lemonade and offered Sophia some. She shook her head. He continued. "My first experience with the way my family works occurred when I was eight. My dad took me down to the basement with him, and he pointed at a man tied in a chair bleeding badly. It was also my first look at Henderson, an imposing man who seemed like a giant to an eight-year-old. Apparently Dad didn't like the way the man in the chair did business. He told me we can't let people control us. As we headed back upstairs, I heard a shot. That's when my childhood ended."

He took a breath. "Jump to ten. I went downstairs to get a drink of water but heard something in the living room. There was my mom with someone other than my dad. She heard me, stopped what she was doing, and hurried over to me. The one thing I remember was her saying, 'it's what we do.' She made it sound like it was okay."

He took another sip of his lemonade. "As I got older, girls flocked to me. I had many girlfriends, but I could never tell if they were there for me or my parents' money."

"It was worse at Stanford. At parties so many underage girls were there, but it wasn't easy to tell their age because of the makeup, the way they dressed—you name it. I met Dr. Boyd's daughter, Kady, at one of those parties when she was seventeen. I have known her since she was thirteen."

He stared out into the darkness. "Everyone thought we made it that night, but we didn't. Her friends brought in the police and then later Kirby, who made it his mission to catch me at any mistake. The problem was my family would cover up any problems our family had, so he was left with nothing and sent packing."

Sophia still had not said anything. Chase continued. "During my first year as an attorney with my family's firm, I spent so much time getting criminals off that it was sickening. Then last fall I decided I was getting out. I sold my Audi, took all the money I had saved, and was even okay with walking anywhere."

He stared at Sophia, realizing for the first time she was wearing slippers. "Dr. Boyd came along, and I took over the bookstore, but not before I figured out my dad had set it up to convince me to move up here for the resort. Of course, I want nothing to do with it. That's when I decided to focus my energies on helping the sheriff with the town's mysteries instead of helping the bad guys."

He patted her hand. "Then I met you and everything changed. I loved you from the moment I first set eyes on you. The problem is I don't want you to see me as a millionaire. I want you to see me as a man who has earned his own way."

He let out a long breath. "Chasing you away with Kirby Hall was my biggest mistake ever. I've been told several times that someday you'll stop waiting for me, and I'll never find true love. My heart tells me I've found love with you. I don't know how any of this makes you feel, but I finally got it off my chest."

She stood up. "I'll take you home now."

They climbed in the car, drove toward the bookstore, and she pulled in back. She shut off the ignition and turned to him. "I will spend the night with you, but nothing will happen between us tonight. I will hold you all night if I need to."

They plodded up the stairs into the living room where Chase dropped onto the couch, feeling drained from all the emotional letdowns.

Sophia peered at him. "Do you need anything?"

"No, I'm good."

She sat down next to him. "Thank you for telling me your story. Please realize it'll never change how I feel about you. I've loved you since the first time I set eyes on you also. And know this: It's not about the money!"

He smiled at her for the first time in a while.

She stared at the ceiling. "Since we're telling our stories, it's my turn. Many considered me a spoiled girl—having everything done for me, getting anything I want, attending large social gatherings at the age of thirteen, traveling around the world. My first modeling experience occurred when I was thirteen when Mom dressed me up in a sexy mini dress, makeup, and big hair, and I walked into the room. Men actually hit on me at that age. Disgusting."

"During high school, boys hit on me, but I was very cautious about who I dated. It was a protective thing for me. At sixteen, I was at a party where a twenty-one-year-old tried to rape me, but Franklin Arthur stepped in and saved me. I was infatuated with him because he was sixteen years older. The next year after I graduated, he became my manager, and I hit the big time moving to San Francisco."

She reached over for his drink. "Please, can I have a drink?"

He handed his lemonade to her. She drained it, jumped up, and poured some more. She sat down next to him once more. "Not only was he my manager, but he also became my lover for several years. Then I got into drugs, especially diet pills to keep my weight down. It started spiraling out of control, then last year I knew I needed to get out of the modeling world, or I'd die."

She took another drink. "Then I met you, which made me want to straighten my life out. The night I saw you kissing Kady devastated me, and I went spiraling into drugs once more. You saw what happened, but I have been clean since and I plan on remaining that way. I reluctantly agreed to marry Kirby and flew out to

Boston because you wanted nothing to do with me. Every day I thought about you and every night I lay in bed thinking about what could have been. I decided it was worth the risk to try to reconnect with you, so here I am."

She trailed a finger down his cheek. "Our lives aren't much different. We can start our lives from here unless I have too much baggage for you, and you'd rather just move on. If that's the case, I know I gave it my best shot, didn't I?"

"I'm sorry I got you out of bed."

"Yes, I was going to sleep."

He reached over and unbuttoned her robe, reaching down to her chest. She gently moved his hand from her chest and interlocked her fingers with his. "It will come but just not tonight. Get some sleep. I'll hold you all night if I need to." She kissed him gently. "One more thing, don't you dare give up your mystery-solving skills. That's who you've become, and I wouldn't change who you are for the world."

Chapter 27

Chase's cell phone vibrated the next morning. He glanced at it, his eyes widening in shock. "It's ten-thirty." He jumped up.

"What's wrong?" Sophia asked through squinting eyes.

"It's ten-thirty and I have to see the sheriff."

She scrambled off the couch. "Yikes, I have a meeting in thirty minutes."

"Weren't you supposed to have breakfast with the Hollands?"

"No, they changed it to lunch, so Mr. Grenham could join them." She kissed him and hurried down the stairs. "I'll see you when I can. Love you."

Before Chase could respond, she was out the door. He finally answered the cell phone. "Are you coming down to the station to talk about what happened yesterday?"

"On my way, Sheriff."

He stripped down, climbed into the shower, and thought about last night. He felt good about getting everything out in the open with Sophia. All that information didn't seem to faze her. He finished his shower, got dressed, and headed to the sheriff's office. He strode in fifteen minutes later.

The receptionist waved him in. "The sheriff is waiting for you."

The sheriff waved him in as Chase started to knock on his door. "Close the door and have a seat."

"What can I do for you?"

The sheriff glanced up at him from fingering through files. "We have a lot to talk about. I was able to talk to Myra Kent, and she gave me a story that I'm having a hard time believing."

"Nothing surprises me, so let me have it."

"She and her boyfriend were part of the mystery hunt. The first night went fine, but then later that night she and her guy heard weird sounds, like someone pounding on the cabin and chanting their names, then just like that it was quiet. They decided to sneak away, to escape. When they opened the door, at least a dozen pairs of eyes were staring at them from the trees, and on the porch was a book with a knife stuck in it."

The sheriff stopped. "I need a drink. Do you want some coffee?"

"Sounds good, Sheriff."

He hit his intercom and ordered two coffees then turned back to Chase. "The chants started once more, and the two hightailed it out of there, running as fast as they could, but they had no clue where they were running to. The chants followed them along the trail. Myra said it was like the voices were herding them where they wanted them to go. Her boyfriend tripped and fell into the hole where he broke his neck immediately, at least that's what she figured from her view from above the deep hole. She never saw him alive again."

There was a knock at the door, and the receptionist came in with two cups of coffee. "Thank you," Chase said.

Once she left, the sheriff continued. "Myra had no idea who was following her or what was going on. The young lady is still scared beyond measure. She and her boyfriend paid $500 apiece for the experience, thinking it would be a fun getaway for them, but it turned out to be a horror show."

"What happened to the other guests?"

"Nowhere to be found. They were the only two left, other than the eyes and the chants. Weird all the way around."

"And the book?"

The sheriff rubbed his beard. "I never asked about the book, but I assumed it was taken by whoever is hosting this mystery hunt. I had a talk with those who participated in the last one, and they said they didn't notice anything different. The weekend went off without a hitch."

"Are we talking about the same group?"

"What do you mean?"

Chase sipped his coffee. "Are the cabins spread out—meaning that one wouldn't know what was happening with another?"

"Myra did say that you couldn't see another cabin because of the trees and mountains that separated each of them. They wanted seclusion."

Chase's mind was racing. "Maybe the others didn't know what was happening because this secluded cabin was away from the others. Did she and her boyfriend choose that one, or did the organizers give it to them?"

"The organizers gave it to them. It sounds like they were targeted."

"Do you know anything about her background?"

"Myra comes from a well-to-do family." The sheriff downed his coffee. "I have an idea, but I'll need your help."

Chase laughed. "You want me to join the next group?"

The sheriff's eyes widened. "How did you know?"

"You're in luck. Before Allison left, she and I bought tickets to the event, so I'm already involved. Now I just have to find a way to convince Sophia to join me."

This time the sheriff laughed. "She'll do anything for you."

"Yeah, but will she do something that could get her killed?"

Chase received a text from Sophia as he walked out of the sheriff's office to let him know she was heading to the bar and grill and to meet her there. He texted he would then walk to the bar and grill. He would always support her any way he could. The bar and grill wasn't too busy when he walked in. He searched the venue but didn't see her. Strange. He walked over to Jake to see if he had seen Sophia.

"She's in the community room in the back with several others."

"Thanks."

He walked in to see a group of people sporting drinks and mingling. Sophia hurried over to him. "I'm glad you're here. There may be some fireworks today because Mr. Holland and Mr. Grenham have been in deep conversations since the two arrived, and my father is not a happy man."

"I'm sorry to hear that."

She grinned. "Yeah, right. How did the meeting with the sheriff go?"

"Weird happenings all the way around. The sheriff wants me to join the next mystery hunt group."

"Does that mean you want me to join you?"

Chase met her eyes. "Would you?"

"Of course, I would. You need someone to watch your back, and why not me?"

"True. What about last night?"

"What about it? Everything is okay. I'm glad we were able to talk about our pasts, and I feel so much better that you know some things about mine." She took his hands. "I told you last night it won't change how I feel about you, ever. In fact, this weekend why don't you join me for a trip to San Francisco? I didn't tell you I have a condo that overlooks the Golden Gate Bridge. It'll be a romantic weekend for the two of us. How about it?"

"It does sound like fun since my birthday is on Sunday."

She grinned. "I may have remembered that. If you agree, I'll book the tickets for Friday afternoon and fly back on Sunday. I have a big meeting on Monday with the Hollands I can't miss. Nor can you."

"Me?"

"Peter Drake is joining them and wants to talk to you about some other stuff. I have no clue what it's about."

They both turned to Mr. Grenham who had joined them. "Chase Connor, it's good to see you once more. How have things been going with you?"

"Between the bookstore and antique shop, things stay pretty busy."

Mr. Grenham stirred his cocktail. "I've heard that. I'm ready to start working with the Native American book distribution whenever you are."

"Great, let's plan on starting it in three weeks."

Mr. Grenham pulled out his phone. "Let me check my calendar to see when I have time." It took a moment before his calendar popped up. "Thursday would be a good day. I'll fly here on Wednesday night, and we can get started the next day."

"Sounds good. I'll set up an open house and invite the press, if you're okay with that?"

"That would be a good idea. I'll have my press secretary contact you to help you with whatever you need. On another note, Mr. Holland told me about what is happening with this technology facility, and I'd gladly talk to the city council on your behalf."

"Thank you, Mr. Grenham," Sophia said. "I know Toby is concerned about my father being involved."

He studied Sophia over his glasses. "You have changed, young lady. Not only are you growing more beautiful every day, but you're also finding your own way in life and not following in your family's footsteps."

She smiled. "Chase and I are working hard not to be like our families and make our own mark in the world."

He patted her on the shoulder. "I'm glad to hear that. Time to go mingle. I understand lunch is ready."

Chase and Sophia joined Mr. Holland and Toby at one table. A few moments later, her father and brother joined them.

Mr. Holland glanced at Sophia. "How is the paperwork coming with the property?"

She put down her drink. "Everything is ready. It just depends on what happens with the city council tonight if they annex the property—"

Nathan Shepherd interrupted. "I'm not sure if that will happen. They are concerned about the four acres."

Mr. Holland eyed Nathan. "Do you really want the four acres that badly?"

Nathan sighed. "It would be good for our bottom line and also for the community."

Mr. Holland looked at his son who nodded. He turned back to Nathan. "Maybe we can work out a contract that is agreeable to all parties concerned."

Nathan finally smiled. "I'm sure we will."

After Chase and Sophia finished their lunch, they went their different ways. It was a busy week for the two of them. They spent the evenings talking to each other, and then Sophia would dash home, only to come back the next morning to cook breakfast for the two of them.

On Friday morning, Chase and Sophia were eating scrambled eggs when he put down his fork. "How can you continue to stay here until midnight, then return before the crack of dawn? Do you ever sleep?"

She put her elbows on the table and gazed into his eyes. "Probably because some guy I know hasn't asked me to move in with him, or better yet, to marry him."

"Heck, if that's all it takes, then why don't you move in with me?"

She grinned. "Nope, I've changed my mind. I'm not moving in with you until you ask me to marry you. I'm fine with this arrangement. Although at times I do enjoy spending the night with you on the couch."

"Did anyone tell you you're weird?"

She spewed out a laugh. "You'd be the first. I should get going because I have a few things to do before we catch our flight. Don't forget a swimsuit. I may have not told you, but I have a hot tub that the two of us can relax in."

That afternoon Chase and Sophia sat in their seats waiting for their plane to take off. Chase glanced at Sophia. "You realize I could have called for the Connor private jet."

She took his hands. "What fun would that be?"

The plane lifted in the air for the first stop at Salt Lake City where they would catch a flight for the final leg to San Francisco. It was seven when they arrived at Sophia's condo.

Sophia opened the door of her condo, grabbed Chase's hand, and pulled him upstairs. "This is the bedroom you can sleep in while you're here. As you can see, it looks over the San Francisco Bay, but then mine does also." She continued showing him the place and didn't let go of his hand the whole time.

He didn't say anything but enjoyed what she was showing him. Chase could tell she was anxious about him being here. He kissed her on the forehead. "Calm down."

She pulled his arm around her and snuggled into his chest. "You're the first person who's ever been in my condo. It's the only place where I feel like I can be myself without having to dress appropriately or meet the needs of my modeling business, family, or friends. No one knows where I go on these trips, and I will keep it that way."

He took her hands and led her to the couch. "Are you going to show me some of your favorite spots around the city?"

She smiled. "I'd enjoy that but not until tomorrow. Tonight, we eat, soak in the hot tub, and see what comes after."

They changed into nice clothes for their dinner out. Chase wore a short-sleeve shirt with denim pants and chestnut-colored comfortable shoes. Sophia dressed in a v-neck minidress with dress sandals.

"You always look so amazing."

She took his hands. "I'm scared since this is the first night we'll actually be on a date together."

"So am I. I don't want to blow it."

She kissed him. "That, my dear, will never happen. Let's enjoy ourselves."

They found a quiet restaurant down around the bridge. Sophia ordered cioppino, a hearty seafood stew, while Chase settled for Liberty farm Peking-style roast duck. They each tasted the other's meal, had glasses of wine, and talked.

"Why do you think Mr. Holland changed his mind about my dad?"

Chase shrugged. "The only thing I can figure is he realized that maybe it would be good to have your father in his corner. Good business sense."

"Yeah, you're probably right."

It was around nine-thirty when they arrived back at Sophia's condo. They changed and stepped down into the hot tub.

"This feels wonderful," Chase said. He pulled Sophia toward him, then wrapped his arm around her.

"I'm glad you're here," Sophia said. "I'm even

more thankful that you're finally in my life, and I'm not letting you out of it."

Ten minutes later, they climbed out and donned fluffy white robes. "Tomorrow will be a busy day, so maybe we should get some sleep," Sophia said, peering into Chase's eyes. "Although I really don't want to. I just want you to hold me all night and never let me go."

He took her in his arms and kissed her. "I am kind of tired myself."

"Then goodnight it is."

The two drifted toward their different bedrooms. He stopped and watched as she disappeared into hers. What was he thinking? He walked toward her room, and knocked gently on the door.

She had just started to pull off her skirt and turned toward him. "Is everything okay?"

"What are we doing here?"

She eyed him. "What do you mean?"

He walked over, lifted her up, and set her gently on the bed.

"You're right, we've waited long enough," she said.

Chapter 28

The next morning Sophia was standing in her robe in front of the stove flipping pancakes. She lifted her head to Chase standing the doorway. "Did you sleep well?" she asked.

"Wonderful. You?"

"I don't know if I even slept, but it's all good. The pancakes are about ready, then I'll show you some of my favorite spots around the area."

Chase grinned. "And maybe find me a pair of shorts."

She laughed. "I'd especially enjoy that."

After breakfast and cleanup, the two browsed in the many stores along the route to grab Chase some shorts and t-shirts. When she wasn't looking, he found a sale on a woman's floppy hat and purchased it for Sophia. He also bought a baseball cap for himself. Chase had her close her eyes and placed the hat on her head. "Now you're styling."

She pulled the hat off her head and grinned. "This is beautiful. Thank you. I see you bought yourself a baseball cap. No Giants or A's?"

"Nope, I don't like either team."

She grinned. "I know you're a Padres fan." She put her hat on, placed her sunglasses back on her face, and linked her arm into Chase's. The two ambled down the trail toward the Bay Bridge. "I usually walk here every day because I love the views, and at night it's beautiful, but I see the sunset from my condo, along with other sights."

She sipped on the drink she had bought while in one of the stores. "We're in Sutro Heights Park, which is an historic public park within the Golden Gate National Recreation Area and Sutro Historic district. As you can see, it offers many places to visit — including Seal Rocks, Ocean Beach, and the Pacific Ocean."

"It is beautiful," Chase said.

The two stopped and sat on a bench to enjoy the views. Sophia pointed. "You can tell that's Seal Beach. Look at all of them."

"Wow, that's cool."

The two strolled the road next to the bay when five minutes later, Sophia stopped behind a painter at his easel. "I want you to meet Fritz. He's a wonderful artist."

"It's been so long, Sophia." The short guy with graying long hair and beard, wearing wire-rimmed glasses hugged Sophia.

She stepped back. "Fritz, I brought a friend to show him your magnificent paintings."

He smiled. "That's sweet, Sophia. Who do we have here?"

"Chase Connor."

Chase proffered his hand. "Nice to meet you. How long have you been painting?"

"All sixty-two years of my life. Has Sophia told

you she loves to paint?"

Chase turned his head to look at her. "No, she hasn't."

"She should. Her paintings are very good, especially the one on the Golden Gate Bridge. I use acrylic paints for my work." He took a drink of his soda.

"I don't know the difference," Chase said.

"The two most popular types of paint used on canvas are oil and acrylic paints. There is a difference. Oil paints offer depth of color, flexibility, and can be applied in different ways, while acrylic paints dry fast, are water soluble, making them easier to clean up." Fritz stopped and shooed away a bird that flew near one of his paintings. "It is also important to choose the right type of canvas. Cotton canvas is a winner, at least in my opinion, because it is an affordable option and the best choice for beginners, but linen canvas lasts longer and is more expensive." He raised a dismissive hand. "There I go, giving you more information than you want."

Chase spoke up. "Could you do a painting of Sophia and me with the Golden Gate Bridge in the background?"

He lifted a shoulder. "I could, but it would take time."

"I'm in no hurry."

"Okay, I'll set up a staged photo and copy it onto the canvas and let you know when I'm finished."

"Great. What do you want us to do?"

Fritz stood up, looked toward the Golden Gate Bridge, using his hands as a viewfinder. "This will be perfect." He pulled out a chair and had Chase sit on it.

"Sophia, why don't you sit on his lap, wrap your arms around his neck, and turn your head toward the camera here?"

They did as he asked, and he took several photos. He showed them to the two, and they both agreed any of the pictures would be fine. "I'll work on the painting when I can and contact Sophia when it's finished."

Chase lifted Sophia off his legs and stood up. "We should let you get back to painting." Once they were on the trail again, Chase linked her arm with his. "That was so cool," he said. "Thank you."

"You're welcome," she beamed.

The two grabbed sandwiches for dinner and sat down on a rock, eating their dinner, and staring out at the bridge. Once they were finished, Chase asked her if she wanted to walk onto the bridge.

"I'd love to. The sidewalk stretches more than two miles and offers cool views of the bay."

The two walked about halfway out to the bridge and stopped to look at the Pacific Ocean. Chase stopped. "Doesn't it feel like we're walking across the sky?"

Sophia looked up at him. "I've never thought about it, but I guess you could say that. Look at all the sailboats, cruise ships, and freighters going to the port. Also there are a lot of birds all the time."

The two were quiet for a long moment as they watched the beauty over the Pacific Ocean. They noticed others standing along the trail enjoying its beauty. Once the sun set, the two headed toward the condo.

When Chase wrapped his arm around Sophia's shoulder, she took his left hand and peered up to him.

"That was gorgeous."

It was past nine when they made it back into the condo. "Do you feel like sitting on the deck with me?"

"Sure," Chase said.

"I'll grab us a couple of lemonades."

Chase stared out at the bridge in the distance until Sophia handed him a glass of lemonade. She pulled a chair closer to him and sat down also. He gazed at her. "Today was a wonderful day."

"It was. I enjoyed walking with you and talking about whatever came to mind. The one thing we both have in common is we haven't been able to find a way to deal with our families."

"I've accepted that it's the way it's going to be."

"Maybe."

Chase pulled out his phone. "I wanted to show you something."

She slid closer to him. Chase found the website he was looking for. "I looked up what price your Golden Gate Bridge painting would go for. Many sell up to $10,000."

"Wow, that's a lot."

He eyed her. "You're doing a wonderful job as a realtor. Have you thought about making painting your profession?"

"Chase, being an artist is tough. Fritz paints all day long and doesn't have a lot to show for it."

"I never said it would be easy, but it would be something you love and are passionate about; that is, if you are interested in it. Anyway, it's something to think about."

"It is."

"Besides, you're already an artist every time you

walk down the runway."

"I'm past all that." She set her iced tea down on a table, did the same thing with Chase's, then crawled on his lap, and wrapped her arms around his neck. She pointed toward the sky. "It is a beautiful sunset, and I want to enjoy it with you."

She laid her head on his shoulder, and they stared into the darkness. "That was one cool day," Chase said.

Sophia shifted his chin to face her, then she kissed him. He responded in kind, unbuttoning her blouse, and gently ran his fingers over her body.

She leaned back and lifted off her shirt.

"Right here on the deck?"

She grinned. "It'll be romantic." Then she shivered.

He stopped and pulled her close to him to keep her warm.

She kissed his nose then his chin. "For the first time ever, I'm with the one man I want to be with. Past, present, future."

He sat back. "You're wrong. I've ruined people's lives. I've broken hearts."

She stroked his cheek. "I brought you here because I want you to see who I am, and I want to find out more about you. Making love is a pleasure that we will always enjoy together. There is no one else I would have wanted to watch over me, hold me, or comfort me after what happened. Please, understand you're the one I'm in love with and want to be with." She framed his face gently with her hands. "Let's just focus on what we're doing."

The next morning Chase's eyes popped open. They were still on the lounge chair on the deck of her condo.

He kissed her on the forehead. She looked so beautiful anytime of the day, but for some reason right now she was radiant.

He grinned as she swiped at the hair in her face. Finally, she opened her eyes, then saw Chase's smile. "How long have you been staring at me?"

"Not long enough. Just for a few minutes."

She reached up, pulled his head down toward her, and kissed him. "Last night was wonderful once more. You're everything I've hoped for in my life."

Chapter 29

Chase couldn't keep his foot from tapping the side of the bench as they waited for the Mountain Ridge City Council meeting to start. Sophia stayed his knee and rolled her eyes.

"Patience," she said. They had sat toward the back to watch all of what was happening.

He huffed and peered around the room. On one side of the room was her father and his contingent of people, while on the other side of the room were the Hollands and a group for Mr. Grenham. Chase whispered. "The battle lines have been drawn."

Sophia couldn't help but laugh. When everyone looked her way, she covered her mouth, and lowered her head. "How embarrassing!"

They all turned to the front when the gavel hit the table signaling the start of the city council meeting. After going over the minutes, the council opened up the discussion on the annexation of the ten acres into the city of Mountain Ridge.

The council president, who was a good friend of Sophia's father's, started the conversation. "Explain to us what is happening here?" he asked the city attorney.

The city attorney, also a good friend of Nathan Shepherd, spoke. "We actually have two requests. One is to annex four acres into the city, while the other is to annex ten acres into the city. The land would go west from the city toward the mountains. The parties are all here who would like to speak on the annexation."

The council president turned to the council members. "Any preference on where to start?"

One council member spoke up. "Let's start with the four-acre plot."

The council president turned to Nathan Shepherd. "Mr. Shepherd, you're up."

Nathan stepped to the podium facing the council. "Thank you, Members of the Council. We thank you for the time to provide input on the four-acre parcel that is next to the city limits. We plan on building a technology center at that location that will be a research facility for a major technology company on the West Coast." Nathan surveyed the room. "The owner of the company is sitting in the crowd, and if you have any questions for him, he'd enjoy answering them. The plan is to build a 2,000-square-foot facility that will house the research equipment along with employing one hundred to one hundred fifty people over the course of three years. Construction would start immediately after all the documents are completed for the annexation. We hope to start the facility by next spring."

After several questions were answered, the city council president turned the floor over to Mr. Holland. He stepped to the podium, surveyed the crowd, then turned to the city council. "Thank you for giving me a few moments to discuss this major project. We're asking for the full ten acres for a major technological complex. It will be a state-of-the-art small technology facility that others could visit and see how something like this can be done in a small community."

He peered once more around the room. "The primary focus at this facility will be research, development, and manufacture of technologically-based goods and services. That was our original idea, but we've expanded that after talking to your local bookstore and antique store owner."

Voices buzzed around the room. The council president hit his gavel. "Calm down, everyone. Let's hear the whole story. Go on, Mr. Holland."

"I'd rather have Mr. Grenham join me up front to discuss his part of this deal."

Mr. Grenham walked up and stood next to Mr. Holland. "First of all, I applaud Mr. Shepherd and his team for what they're trying to accomplish, and whatever the council decides we will support. Mr. Holland and I will continue to make a commitment to Mountain Ridge as well as to Flathead County. Mr. Holland's expansion ideas stem from a conversation that I had with Chase Connor recently, and believe me, the city council was difficult, because I have no liking for the Connor family, but Chase made me sit up and listen. I gave him two minutes, and his pitch took only one minute, but it was a good one."

He turned to search the crowded council room. "Chase, please come up here?"

Chase frowned. Sophia pushed him. "Go, tell them what you told me."

Chase slowly walked up to the podium. "Council, those in the room, thank you for taking a few moments of your time to listen to what is happening here. The conversation Mr. Grenham is referring to took place at one of the many social events that, as a business owner, I participate in." He really didn't like the fact they had caught him off guard. "I really hate standing in front of people talking about ideas that people more qualified than myself should be explaining. My idea involves the Native American culture, and I'm glad that Mr. Bottoms, along with several other members of the local tribe, are here because the Native American culture is prominent in this area. There is just so much we don't know about their culture, and that's sad. I'm proposing to start reading classes in the bookstore and on the reservation that would bring the Native American culture into focus. Granted there are books on Native Americans in both locales, but there is little discussion between the two groups of what the culture is all about.

He could feel himself getting into the spirit. "For instance, we could start with cookbooks from both cultures and offer small plates at kiosks where people could sample the different recipes. Imagine a variety of booth displays in the convention center, on the reservation, or even on the streets of the county communities."

Mr. Holland joined in. "We've decided to take this one step further by making a specific wing for Native American technology programs where those on the reservation can come and learn how to do technological research, everything associated with the field, and make a career of their own. It won't just be a technological research center; it'll also be a starting point for new businesses. We'll take any questions."

One council member spoke up. "You could expand any of your businesses to fulfill that need. Why here?"

"Two key elements. Lower costs and new jobs to the Mountain Ridge area," Mr. Holland said. "There could be as many as two to three hundred jobs, as well as start-up technology programs for the Native Americans and others who live in Flathead County—"

The council president interrupted. "Have you and Mr. Shepherd had discussions on these issues?"

Mr. Holland nodded. "Our philosophies differ, but we're still willing to work with Mr. Shepherd and his group, but only under circumstances where we're all in agreement. At this point Mr. Shepherd and I are not in agreement with what direction we're going in."

The council president looked around at the council members. "Any other questions?" There were none. He then peered out at the crowd. "Any thoughts?" When there were none, he turned back to the council. "It's time for the vote."

One of the council members recommended the ten acres be annexed in order for Mr. Holland to develop his project. There was a second. The vote was unanimous. The council president turned to Mr. Holland. "We'll get the annexation process underway," the council president said.

Applause filled the room. Chase and Sophia watched as her father stormed out. "I guess he didn't like the outcome," Chase said.

Sophia smacked him lightly on the shoulder. "Don't be like that. But it'd probably be good that I stay at your place tonight."

"You're always welcome."

Hours later, the two sat on the couch holding each other and drinking wine. "This is a wonderful thing that's happening," Chase said.

"It is. I'm so proud of what you've accomplished. You are not your family, and tonight you proved it once more. That's why I love you so much. You care about so many things."

"Especially you."

She leaned back and unbuttoned her shirt. "Why don't you show me how much you care about me?"

Chapter 30

Chase and Sophia arrived at the pickup point for the mystery hunt on Friday afternoon. Waiting for them were several others they recognized; some they didn't.

Brink walked over to Chase. "You're here. Are you looking forward to the weekend?"

"I am," Chase said. "You know Sophia Shepherd."

Brink grinned, showing a couple of missing teeth. "Everyone knows Sophia Shepherd. It's nice to see you again, Sophia."

"And you too, Brink. Where's Olivia?"

Brink frowned. "She and I broke up a few weeks ago. Everything changed after we went through the house, and after what happened with that big guy. This weekend I'm part of the group who will be helping out."

They turned when a van showed up. "It's time to load up," Brink said.

Everyone climbed onto the van, grabbed a seat, and then drove north toward the mountain. The guide explained that they would travel to a point, then climb onto horses for the remainder of the ride up the mountain. "It's a one-hour ride up alternating slopes and cliffs. It provides an amazing view of the mountain, valleys, and wildlife."

Twenty minutes later the van pulled into a spot. Sophia tapped Chase's shoulder. "The cabin we were at."

Chase nodded. "The journey is about to begin."

They all climbed out of the van where several people were waiting for them. A large man smiled. "I'm Ezekiel Boyen, and I'll be your trail guide up the mountain to the site where the weekend begins. Plan on a wonderful experience."

Horses were assigned to the group which consisted of twenty people, ten males and ten females. They climbed on their horses, and the guide started up the trail on the mountain. Ezekiel led the group, and there were three other riders leading the pack, including one that brought up the rear.

Chase noticed every detail as they wound up the mountain. Ezekiel stopped them twice before they reached the area where the cabins were. He waved his arm. "This will be your home for the weekend. Cabins have been assigned to you and your significant other."

Chase and Sophia followed the guide toward a cabin that was near a small creek but away from most of the others. "Why so isolated?" Chase asked.

Ezekiel's expression didn't change. "This is the number you were given when you signed up. If you want to change it, I'll see what I can do."

"We're good. I was just asking."

He smiled. "Good. Dinner and a campfire will begin in an hour giving you time to freshen up and take care of whatever other needs you have."

Chase noticed Ezekiel's eyes remained on Sophia a moment too long. She cringed. "Is that all?" Chase asked.

Ezekiel turned his attention back to Chase. "Yeah, that's it."

Once he left, Sophia glanced at Chase. "He gives me the willies."

"He is a bit strange. Let's settle in."

It was six when Chase and Sophia joined the others at a large campfire in the center of a ring. Others had already gathered around it, drinking, smoking some kind of drug, and laughing. Brink joined the two. "You decided to show up."

Chase patted his stomach. "We're kind of hungry."

Brink tilted his head to another area. "The food and drink is over there."

"Thanks," Sophia said.

She took Chase's hand, and they headed toward the buffet line where several others were already filling their plates. Chase grabbed a couple of paper plates, handed Sophia one, and they went through the line filling their tray with vegetables, pork sandwiches, and lemonades. They found a place around the fire to sit and watch what was happening. After they ate, many started dancing and singing to the loud rock music that was playing. That went on for a couple of hours before the people started filtering toward their cabins.

Chase turned to Sophia. "Should we head back to the cabin?"

She grinned. "I'm feeling..." She stopped what she was going to say and just batted her eyes.

He laughed. An hour later they were in bed when they started hearing noises around the cabin...the sound of beating against trees or logs, then shrill screams and a bevy of loud voices. Chase climbed out of bed, slipped on his shorts, and opened the door. Nobody was there, but eyes glimmered from the trees all around. They seemed to be staring at the cabin.

He peered down onto the deck and saw a book of sorts with a knife stuck into it. He ran over to it and pulled the knife off, and picked up the book. The voices were getting louder. He set the book back down, and the voices lowered. The eyes continued staring at him. What was going on?

He gasped at Sophia's touch. She was still in her robe. "What's happening?"

"I'm not sure. I found this book down here with this knife stuck in it, and those eyes." He motioned with his head. "They seem to be staring at me."

Sophia turned to see, then wrapped her arms around her chest. "They sure are haunting." She took his hand. "Come, back to bed."

He grabbed the book, then took one last glance at the eyes in the trees before locking the door. Chase couldn't fall asleep, so he turned on the light and opened the book. It was a diary or a journal of some kind. He started reading.

We heard someone or something beating on the walls of the cabin, then the chanting started. It grew so loud that it made our ears ring for many minutes. When we couldn't take anymore, we dressed, and stormed out of the cabin. There waiting for us were at least a dozen sets of eyes staring at us. Then the voices started once more. The volume rose higher and higher, causing our eardrums to feel like they were bursting. Covering our ears, we raced away from the cabin toward the mountain. Every time we turned around, the eyes stared at us and the shrill voices got louder. It was like the eyes were steering us toward the mountaintop. We reached the summit with nowhere to go. The eyes encircled us, then one voice spoke our names. We had only one course of action—jump!

Chase peered up from the book. How and why was the book left on their doorstep? Was this a warning? Were they next? Chase rushed to the bed and shook Sophia. Her eyes popped open. "Get dressed and grab everything."

She rubbed her eyes. "You're scaring me, Chase."

"I just read this diary, and I believe it's a warning for us. We need to move out and quickly."

Sophia jumped out of bed, got dressed, and packed her things. Meanwhile, Chase made sure he had certain items in his backpack close at hand. He stopped when the pounding started again. This time the voices and the pounding were just outside the door.

He switched his attention to Sophia. "The trek may be hard. Make sure you put on jeans, tennis shoes, and your jacket."

Several minutes later they were ready. The pounding and voices had stopped. Chase opened the door and searched the area. The eyes were still staring at them. Just like that the voices started calling their names.

A bullet whipped past his head and hit the cabin door. Sophia peered out. "Are they shooting at us?"

"It seems like it. Are you ready?"

She nodded. Chase took her hand. "We're about ready to find out what this mystery hunt is all about. Keep your head down."

Chase donned the backpack and dashed around the back of the cabin where more eyes glared at them.

"They seemed to know where we can or can't go," Sophia said.

"Or they're pointing us in the direction they want us to go. Let's see where they take us."

They hurried up the trail, stopping every few minutes to check behind them. The eyes were still behind them. Finally, they reached the end of the trail and stared down at a rapid river. When Chase turned to retrace his steps, he saw the eyes once more.

Chase hollered. "What do you want with us?"

The voices went silent, and then a masked man stepped out from between the eyes. "Chase Connor, Sophia Shepherd, your time has come."

Chase took a step toward the man with the mask. "What do you mean?"

"You helped criminals to go free. You're a cad who left a woman for another. Sophia's family has ruined this county. The list of your deeds goes on and on. The world is better off without either of you."

Chase stepped back at the sight of several rifle muzzles pointed on them. He pulled Sophia close to him and whispered in her ear. "I love you." Just like that he took her hand, and the two jumped down into the river below.

Shots bellowed as he fell into the river with Sophia. The two separated as they struggled to keep their heads above the racing water. In the distance Chase heard her screams as he battled to grab a breath in the midst of the burgeoning waves. Did the current pull her underneath? Had he ruined another life as the man had said?

He grabbed a branch—a lifeline as the current pulled him down. Voices sounded from up on the mountaintop, punctuated by bullets pelting the water around him. His muscles tore as he fought to hold onto the branch and pull himself toward the bank. Five minutes later, out of breath, he made it to land, finding Sophia lying there inert. He hurried over to her and shook her.

"Are you okay?"

Her eyes flickered open, and she retched, water spewing out. She lifted onto her elbow, trying to catch her breath. Finally, she lifted her head. "Next time…warn me…before we jump off…a cliff."

He smiled. "You are gorgeous." He kissed her gently, then more passionately when she responded.

Moments later she pushed back, shivering, her lips blue. "Really? Right here and now?" Noises came from the mountain above. Chase peered up at it. "They've found a trail," Chase said. "We really need to find a place to change out of these wet clothes. Of course everything's wet now."

He climbed off the bank, took her hand to pull her up, and they ran through the trees toward the mountains. They had traveled for at least thirty minutes when they found an opening. They slowly climbed the narrow trail to the opening.

"It's a cave. We may be safe here, or at least it will give us a chance to catch our breath to come up with a plan. Let's get out of these wet clothes. Gather all the wood or anything else you can find that will burn."

"Won't the fire bring them to us?" Sophia asked.

"I have a feeling they are going to find us sooner rather than later. We need to get warm, or we won't stand a chance. They know the area better than we do, but we did win the first round."

Once they stripped down to their drawers, Sophia hung the clothes on the rocks. She snuggled close to Chase who sat next to the small fire. "What are we going to do?"

Chase focused his attention on the cave entrance. "We're going to do everything we can to stay ahead of them until we can find some help."

Chapter 31

Chase's eyes popped open. Sophia hadn't moved the whole night. Remaining immobile, he kept his eyes focused on the trail outside the cave. He gently shook Sophia who opened her eyes. "Let's get dressed. Someone's coming this way."

She hurried over to the clothes and slipped into hers. "Here you go."

Chase took the clothes and put them on. They both froze at the crunch of a broken branch.

"Where could they have gone? Let's check this cave."

Chase whispered into Sophia's ears, "Hide in the corner. Grab a few rocks and be ready to use them. He quickly doused the fire, knowing the smoke would give them away He joined her in the darkest corner.

One of the searchers stuck a head through the cave entrance. Once he noticed the firepit, he hollered back to his partner. Both came into the cave to check out the fire. One spoke. "The embers are still burning. We must have just missed them." They spun around and left. Once they were out and their footsteps ebbed, he took Sophia's hand. "Now's our chance to get out of here," he whispered.

"Where can we go?" she whispered back.

He hugged her. "We'll get through this. You and I have a life to live, and no one will stop us from that." Chase peeked outside of the cave to see. When he saw no movement, he grabbed Sophia's hand and hurried through the trees. They stopped twenty minutes later to catch their breath.

"Do you have any ideas where we're at?" Chase said, bent over.

Trying to catch her breath, Sophia just shook her head.

Their heads both popped up at the sound of voices. Chase pulled her back into the bush as two people walked by. They stopped in front of them to search the area.

One person lifted his mask. "Why are we wearing these things? They're hot and it's hard to see."

"Quit complaining," the other guy said.

They searched for a few minutes more before finally leaving the area. Once they were out of sight, Sophia whispered to Chase. "I've heard that voice before. It sounded like a man who hung out with Willis before he got into trouble and wound up in jail."

Chase was quiet. He looked at Sophia. "It's safe to say this group has been involved with the law in the past." They walked through the trees and came to a trail. Chase took her hand, and they inched along keeping their eyes peeled for anything out of the ordinary.

"Despite the danger, this is beautiful," Sophia said.

"I agree."

They walked for another mile when Chase stopped

suddenly. Ahead were several all-terrain vehicles alongside a cabin.

"You might as well join us."

They turned to a man in a mask who trained a gun at Chase. "Pretty impressed you were able to lose us for more than a day. But then the boss said you were resourceful."

Chase stared behind the man which drew the man's attention. He turned his head just a bit to see what Chase was looking at. Chase barreled into the man knocking him down.

"Run, Sophia." Chase kicked the man in the face, causing blood to spew out his nose.

"Damn it, you broke my nose."

Chase scooped up his rifle and dashed toward where Sophia had headed. Other voices hollered, "After him."

Chase made it to the trees where Sophia was waiting for him. He grabbed her hand. "We have to go." They maneuvered the best they could through the thick forest. The voices were finally gone. Chase stopped so they could catch their breath.

Sophia glared at him. "That man had a gun pointed at you. What were you thinking?"

"Getting away from him."

He took her hand, and they started walking once more. Another thirty minutes Chase stopped. "We have good cover here." He shifted her toward him. "I'm sorry I scared you. It was a reaction that got us the rifle. It also gave me an idea."

"What are you thinking?"

Chase reached into his backpack and grabbed a couple of protein bars with his canteen of water. "We need to keep our strength up."

As they were eating, Chase explained his plan. "We hopefully can wind our way back to those vehicles, grab one, and hightail it down the mountain."

"That's pretty risky."

He downed a gulp of water. "I know but I hope they won't expect it."

She pulled him toward him and planted a hard kiss. "That's for luck."

He pulled her up. "Let's try to get there by dark."

The sun started to set when they arrived at the cabin from a different direction. Chase slid down on the ground. "Now we wait."

Sophia slid down next to him, and soon gentle snores ensued. He gently stroked her hair. "You're such a gamer." Chase kept his eyes alert. Several times he saw people checking their vehicles, a couple even driving away. One drove by the tree line shining his light into the trees. Chase knew they wouldn't be seen. The vehicle disappeared.

Finally, everything settled down and the lights went out in the cabin. Chase waited a bit longer to make sure everything was quiet. It was another hour before Chase gently shook Sophia. Her eyes popped open. "It's time," Chase whispered.

The two moved quietly through the trees. At the tree line's edge, Chase stopped to listen to any sound in the nights. Nothing other than the normal animal calls reached his ears. He whispered into Sophia's ear. "Take this rifle and point it at the cabin entrance. Anyone opens that door; you just start firing. Don't stop."

Her eyes widened. "What if I hit someone?"

He took her head in his hands. "They are trying to

kill us. Do you understand?"

She nodded.

"Okay, I'm going to get us a terrain vehicle. Be ready."

"Please be careful."

He smiled. "You just have to be ready."

Chase quietly made his way down to the all-terrain vehicle sitting on the edge. He searched and found the key under the floor mat. He prayed it would start and it did. The lights in the cabin popped on. He steered toward Sophia. "Let's go for a ride."

She climbed on the back and Chase drove toward the trail. The voices of people reached them. Chase veered the vehicle down the side of the mountain in the dark.

"Do you have any idea where you're going?" Sophia said.

He turned his head a bit. "Yes, I remember the trail that brought us up this way on the horses. It was fairly open."

Ten minutes later, Sophia peered back. "Lights coming from behind. They're gaining on us."

"Hold on."

Chase gunned the vehicle pushing it to its limits, as they careened down the mountain not for sure where they were going or if the trail was open. Sophia pointed to the left ahead of them. "It looks like a fork in the trail."

Chase saw it and hit a hard right, tipping the vehicle on its side, but Chase pulled the steering wheel to the left, bringing it back under control.

Sophia had moved to the seat next to his and buckled her seatbelt. Her head swiveled behind them.

"They kept going, not able to make the turn, or they didn't notice us turning. I think we've lost them for now."

Ahead was another cabin with an old truck. Chase brought the vehicle to a stop. They jumped out and ran toward the cabin. Chase pounded on the door, and it opened shortly after. A man who stood taller than Chase with a white beard and hair down to his waist trained a gun at them.

"What are you two doing out here at three in the morning?"

Chase tried to catch his breath. "We're being hunted."

"Are you Chase Connor?"

Chase didn't say anything for a moment. "If I am?"

The man smiled. "Edgar told me to help you any way I could. But I can't help you if you don't get rid of that vehicle." He leaned his rifle against the door. "I'll help you."

Chase jumped off the porch, ran over to the jeep, and grabbed the keys to start it up. The man touched his shoulder. "No, they'll hear it. There is a ravine right behind my cabin. We can push it over into the ravine, and that's where they'll find the vehicle. They won't know until morning if you survived or not, but by that time I'll have taken you down the mountain so you can get help. I have no communications up here."

They struggled but they were able to push the vehicle over the edge of the cliff down into the ravine. They watched as it exploded on impact. The man touched Chase's arm. "Come with me. They'll be here soon."

They hustled back into the cabin. The man quickly

moved the couch away from the wall. He reached down and opened a door. "Down there is a wine cellar. You'll be safe for now."

Once the two had climbed down the small ladder, they looked up as the man pulled the couch over them.

Sophia squeezed into Chase. "Do you think anyone will believe us when we tell them what happened tonight?"

"I don't believe I drove an all-terrain vehicle fifty miles an hour in the dark on a shallow path and I didn't kill us."

She grinned. "You have skills."

Chapter 32

The man was staring at the fire down below when he turned and saw Ezekiel Boyen standing next to him.

"What happened, Winter Graze?"

The man called Winter Graze turned to Ezekiel. "I have no clue. I heard something roar past my cabin, jumped out of my bed, ran outside, and saw whatever it was go over the mountain. I saw the explosion as soon as it hit."

"Was anyone in the vehicle?"

"It sure looked like it, but I can't be too sure since it was so dark. What are you doing out this late anyway?"

Ezekiel continued staring at the fire down below. "We had an incident at the mystery hunt. Two people stole some money from the head camp, then stole one of the all-terrain vehicles, and it looks like this is where they ended."

"It seems like you have a lot of problems at your mystery hunt each year."

"It's really none of your business," Ezekiel said.

"You realize you'll have to call this in," Winter

Graze said.

Ezekiel glared at the man. "Yeah, I guess we will." Ezekiel stormed away from Winter Graze, climbed onto the back of an all-terrain vehicle, and disappeared into the night. Winter Graze kept his eye on the direction he went, knowing the guy may turn around and come back at any time.

Then another fifteen minutes passed by, and nothing happened. Winter Graze was satisfied that the man had left. He hurried back into his cabin, moved the couch, then lifted up the door. "He's gone."

Sophia climbed up the ladder followed by Chase. "We'll never be able to thank you enough for what you've done," Chase said.

The man smiled. "Edgar wouldn't be too happy with me if I wouldn't have helped Chase Connor or what everyone refers to as 'the mystery man.'"

Sophia returned the smile. "What is your name?"

"I go by Winter Graze. My real name is Simon Blacktail, but I go by my Kootenai name. You can call me Simon. We can talk later, but right now we have to get you down the mountain before Ezekiel figures out you're alive."

"Won't he have to call the authorities?" Sophia asked.

Simon eyed her. "He won't because then it will blow whatever he has going on up there. Right now, he'll be moving everyone out of there and cleaning everything up."

Sophia sensed something in Chase. "No, you don't, Chase."

Chase took Sophia's hand. "Someone has to stop it."

"Then I'm going with you."

Simon jumped in. "I'll go with him. You take my pickup. Drive down to a small cabin about a quarter of a mile where Mrs. Abigail will let you use her phone."

"At four in the morning?" Chase asked.

Simon nodded. "She's just getting off work now. You had better get going."

Chase wrapped his arms around Sophia. "I told you we had a whole life to live."

She kissed him hard. "I'll hold you to that."

Simon gave her the keys to the truck. She kissed Chase one more time, then hurried out the door. Simon patted Chase's back. "I see a woman who's in love. We had better keep you alive. Now we need to hurry if we want to disrupt their cleanup of everything."

~

They moved quickly through the trees. Chase noticed that Simon knew exactly where he was going. Within thirty minutes the cabins were in sight, and everyone was hustling to clean up.

Chase and Simon viewed the situation. "They're efficient," Chase said. "It's like they know exactly what needs to be done and have done this many times. If I didn't know any better, I would think they're former military."

"They're a lot of those in the mountains so it's possible. Right now, we need to disrupt their activities so the authorities can arrive."

"How do you expect to do that?"

Simon pointed. "The woodpile. If we can set that on fire, it'll slow them down a bit. Despite how egregious they are, no one wants to set the mountains on fire."

"How do we start a blaze and keep it going?"

Simon grinned, pulling out a bottle of whiskey from inside his coat. "For special occasions. Let's go."

Simon led him through the trees toward the firewood which sat a safe amount of distance away from a cabin. He handed Chase the bottle after he took one drink. Chase poured the remainder of the bottle on the logs, lit the matches, then a minute or two later the logs went up in flames.

Five minutes later someone noticed the flames. There was hollering and scrambling around to try to stop the fire which was reaching the nearest cabin. While they were battling the fire, Simon disappeared into another cabin. He arrived back several minutes later with a bag.

"This will slow them up indefinitely. It's cash."

Simon opened it to show Chase a full bag of greenery. "How much do you think is in there?" Chase asked.

"Thousands if not tens of thousands." He shook his head at Chase's wide eyes. "This scam of a mystery hunt is only about money."

Over the next hour, they watched as the group battled the blaze. Then a chopper hung above them shining a large light on them. "Drop everything. You're all under arrest."

Another chopper arrived. Men slid down on ropes to the ground.

Simon grinned. "The Mounties have arrived to make some arrests."

The mystery crew scattered trying to escape but were easily rounded up by the men from the chopper. A man darted toward the trees behind him. "Is that

Ezekiel?"

"It sure is."

Chase ran after him. He was going to make sure this man did not escape. He was almost upon him when Ezekiel quickly veered to his right. Chase followed as quickly as he could in the dark. Ezekiel had one advantage. He knew the forests better than Chase.

Ten minutes later Chase had lost the man. He stopped to catch a breath, searching the area the best he could in the dark. Just then something smashed against him knocking him to the ground. Ezekiel twisted him around and pummeled Chases's face "You ruined this whole operation," Ezekiel said. "Now you're going to pay with your life."

Chase managed to stop the barrage of fists, kicking the man off him. Ezekiel tried to scramble up off the ground, but Chase grabbed his ankle, and Ezekiel fell flat on his face. Chase jumped up, ready for what would happen next.

Like a cat, Ezekiel bounded off the ground, pulled out a knife, and waved it at Chase. Chase dodged back as the wildcat thrust the knife toward him. "I should have killed you when I had the chance, but you're not going to escape this time."

He sliced Chase's arm with a single jab, then sprang toward him. Chase sidestepped as Ezekiel fell past him. The shorter man got up once more and came after him. Chase launched himself toward Ezekiel, and his full weight knocked him back to the ground, the knife falling off to the right.

Chase wrapped his arm around the man's neck and squeezed. Ezekiel struggled for a few minutes then the kicking subsided. Chase let go hoping he hadn't killed the guy. He peered up as two rifles were pointed at him. "You can let him go now, Chase."

Chase lifted his head toward the voice. "Sheriff Portal, it's nice to see you." Chase staunched the blood in his arm as the sheriff put cuffs on Ezekiel.

"This is far from over, Connor," the wildcat glared at Chase.

The sheriff pushed him forward. "Let's go join the others. Chase, you need to get that arm checked."

Chase tarried a bit behind the sheriff and Ezekiel. Once at the cabin area, Chase sat down on one of the cabin porches watching law enforcement do their job. Simon joined him. "Well, Chase, it seems like everything is being taken care of perfectly."

They both glanced up when an EMT joined them. "The sheriff told me you may have been cut up. Let's see what's happening."

Chase stretched out his right arm. The EMT sniffed. "Just a scratch. You'll be just fine. I'll clean it up and wrap it, but you need to make sure it doesn't get infected, and wrap it."

Over the next couple of minutes, the EMT went to work. "That should help it," he said, finishing putting the wrapping on.

"Thanks," Chase said.

The EMT dashed to check out others. Ten minutes later the sheriff joined the two. "Nice work. Quite an operation it seems they had going on up here. Many of the helpers are already spilling their guts hoping not to serve any jail time. A couple of them are pretty tight-lipped, but we have enough to break up this racket for good."

Simon spoke. "I'm glad you finally were able to

catch these guys. They've created havoc over the last couple of years in the mountains. I've called your office several times, but nothing ever happened."

The sheriff sighed. "We never had anything to go on, but now we do, and we'll make sure these guys do their time. I'll give you two a lift down the mountain."

Chase eyed him. "How did you get up here in the dark?"

The sheriff grinned. "I know how to handle an ATV."

Chapter 33

The sun was rising when a parade of ATVs carried the guilty parties associated with the mystery hunt down from the mountain. In all, there were fifteen people who were arrested. There were different charges bestowed on the group from misdemeanors to felony attempted murder charges. Ezekiel was charged with one count of murder and three other counts of attempted murder, along with embezzlement and money laundering.

Chase and Sophia shifted uncomfortably in the waiting room of the county law enforcement building waiting to be interviewed by the sheriff. Portal always made it a point to interview Chase involving any incident.

Chase peered at Sophia. "One thing I don't understand is how they made their eyes glow like that at night. Mountain lions can do that because they have a reflective layer of tissue behind the retina, but humans can't."

Sophia frowned. "Hm. Did you notice the different colors around their eyes? My guess is they were using some type of shimmering eyeshadow which would make their eyes sparkle and glow. Another thing. Flashlights could help contribute to their eyes shining. Of course, at night everything is perception because it's dark out."

Sophia laid her head down on Chase's shoulder. "I'm so tired I could sleep for a week."

"I'm just glad this is over, and we can move forward with our lives."

She lifted her head. "And what may that include, my dear?"

"Everything you've wanted in your life—marriage, children, a new house."

"Hold it, I never said I wanted a new house. I love your two-room apartment above the bookstore."

He gently tipped her head toward him with his finger. "Explain how you're going to raise six children in that apartment?"

She grinned. "We spend more time on the couch than in the bed."

Chase didn't answer right away. She must have noticed. "What is it?"

"Maybe we should consider moving back to California."

She lifted her head off of his shoulder and glanced at him. "I do have the condo we could live in, but why would you even consider that?"

"Look at what just happened over the last twenty-four hours. We jumped into a raging river some five hundred feet down from a mountain, we were shot at by crazies, and a guy almost gutted me."

She sat up, climbed onto his lap, then peered into his eyes. "I hear everything you say, but tell me if our lives wouldn't be in danger in California. You've told me a couple of times as we've lain in bed together that everyone wanted a piece of the Connors, and that's why you were hesitant about marrying me. It doesn't matter where we live if that's the case." She kissed him on the forehead. "I'm not leaving you, no matter what happens. If you choose to go to California, I'll be right there with you. If you stay here, it'll be the same. I love you with all my heart." She kissed him tenderly at first, then passion took over. They both turned to a cough. Sophia quickly buried her head in Chase's shoulder when they saw the sheriff.

"How come every time I need to talk to either one of you, you're kissing or doing something goofy like that?"

Chase shrugged. "I can't help it. We love each other. I'm sure you and your loved one do it also."

"But not in public."

"You should try it. Who's next?" Chase asked.

"Let's go, Sophia."

A couple of hours later, Chase and Sophia trudged up the stairs into the bedroom and crashed on the bed fast asleep. They didn't wake up until the next morning when the cell phone rang.

A groggy Chase answered it. "Hello."

"Good morning. You realize it's nine, and you should be up."

"Okay, Sheriff, what can I do for you?"

"Kind of crabby, aren't you?"

"Yeah, it's been a long twenty-four hours."

"It's going to get longer because Ezekiel broke out of jail last night, and he's gunning for you."

Chase quickly turned and saw that Sophia was not lying next to him. "How would you know that?"

"Inmates heard a conversation, so I'm sending a deputy to watch over you two."

"Sheriff, it's too late."

Chase turned to the man standing in his bedroom doorway. "Okay, tell the sheriff goodbye," Ezekiel said.

"Got to go," Chase said, hanging up on the sheriff.

"Let's get dressed. We have a long ride ahead of us." He looked around. "Where's the Shepherd girl?"

Chase lied. "I wouldn't know where she is. We just happened to be there together that night."

Ezekiel spew out a huff. "No matter. You're the one I want. We can end it here or in the mountains. It's your choice."

"First explain to me why you want me dead so badly?"

The man chuckled. "Simple, I was pulling in millions of dollars with my elaborate game, but you had to go and ruin it."

"How could that happen when people were either disappearing or dying?"

He grinned. "We targeted those who were rich and who could provide us with the ransom money. It was too bad about the woman who fell and broke her ankle. She slipped away, kind of like you did. Now let's go."

"At least can I get dressed?"

"Where you're going it won't matter, but it probably would be good to wear a T-shirt and those sandals on the floor."

Chase reached down for the sandals. As he lifted his head up, Sophia bashed Ezekiel on the side of the head with a cast-iron skillet. A shot went off and Chase fell onto the bed.

~

Sophia hurried over to him and moaned. "No. No. Not now, Chase. Not after I finally have you in my life."

Chase sat up. "He nicked my arm. Is he dead?"

"I hope so, but I think he's still breathing. I hit him at least three times to make sure he was out. Let me see the arm." She ran to the bathroom to grab some gauze and a wet rag, scrambling back out. Once she cleaned the wound, she wrapped it with gauze. "You're going to be all right."

"I'm just glad you weren't still in bed."

She sighed as she finished wrapping it. "I couldn't sleep, so I tiptoed out to take a walk, and when I came back upstairs, the door was open a bit. I know I hadn't left it open. I slipped in, heard his voice, saw the skillet on the stove. You saw the rest."

He pulled her close and kissed her. "We've been through a lot together. Can you open the top drawer and grab a box? Both my arms are too damaged to do so."

Once she retrieved the box, she handed it to Chase. He opened it and pulled out a Montana sapphire ring.

"I bought this last year with the hopes of putting it on your finger someday. Then you were gone, and the day passed, so I gave it to Allison. But now it is that day, and I hope you're not disappointed that someone wore it before you." He slid it on her finger.

"I'm not disappointed. It's beautiful."

She kissed him once more. He pulled out another ring. "This is not the engagement ring I gave to Allison. It's one I bought specifically for you. After all we've been through, I just hope that you'll still want to marry me."

Tears flowed down her cheeks. "I accept."

He placed it on her finger and kissed her. Both turned to a cough. Chase and Sophia both laughed. "It seems like you always show up at the most inappropriate times," Chase grinned.

"With you two, who knows what I'll see."

Sophia showed him her left hand. "Today you'll find that this guy finally decided to ask me to marry him, and despite what you see on the floor, I accepted."

"Congratulations. Although it doesn't surprise me since everyone in the county knew you two were heading in that direction. I hate to say this, but you two are made for each other. So will someone explain to me what happened here?"

Sophia grabbed the skillet. "He had a gun pointed at Chase, and I just started pounding on his head with this skillet. I don't think he's dead, but he'll have a big headache."

The sheriff laughed. "I'd agree."

They turned to Ezekiel who was groaning. "What hit me?"

The sheriff slapped handcuffs on his wrists. "You ran into the Connors."

THE END

Other books by this author
<u>Hidden in the Book, Map of the Lost, Book 1</u>
<u>Bouncing Back</u>
<u>The Battle Off the Court</u>
<u>Freedom Flight</u>
<u>Fight for Survival</u>
<u>Road to Hell</u>
<u>A New Life Begins</u>
<u>Relentless</u>
<u>Missing</u>
<u>Targeted</u>

Author Bio: My wife, Susan and I have two sons, Justin (Kayla) and Jeremy and a grandson, Aiden. Born and raised in South Dakota. I enjoy spending time with family, traveling and putt-putt. I recently retired as managing editor of a small town Iowa newspaper. I am a former Marine Corps veteran, getting my start in the publishing business in 1981 working for several years on base newspapers. I spent time running my own freelance business. I love writing. I enjoy reading anything and everything. I also love the history of our country and enjoy reading western books, mysteries, and adventure novels, and watching mystery, adventure, and western movies.

9 781965 352205